LUCIFER'S
Sin

NEW YORK TIMES BESTSELLING AUTHOR
LISA RENEE JONES

ISBN-13: 979-8421575535

www.lisareneejones.com

CHAPTER ONE

Ana

My head is killing me, which is probably because I spent the evening dishonoring my FBI badge by listening in while a senator entertained his side chick. How is this my job? *Why* is this my job? At twenty-six, and with three years on the job, somehow, this is not the dream anymore. Meanwhile, my partner, Darius, laughed his way through the "show" and stuffed his face with French fries with zero concern as to what was going on inside the agency we work for. Or the fact that Senator Pike is an asshole, but from what we've both seen over the past three months, he's not breaking the law, just his marriage. Why are we even monitoring him? Obviously, someone knows something I'm not privy to, which is all too often the case.

I pull into the parking lot of the convenience store near my house with the intent of grabbing something for my headache. Once I've parked near the door, I step outside into the chilly night. Beautiful, fat snowflakes are fluttering about, here and there, reminding me why I love winter in Colorado. It also makes me happy I'm in street clothes that include jeans and a turtleneck sweater.

My boots crunch on gravel as I walk toward the entrance of the store. I'm almost there when a car speeds up and screeches to a halt. The passenger's door pops open and the hair on the back of my neck stands up. A man exits the store, a gun in his hand, and all but lunges for the vehicle.

Adrenaline courses through me and I draw my weapon, but it's too late to stop what is in motion. The man is already inside the car, and it's moving. I jog after it, trying to catch a plate number, only to discover there isn't one. Seconds could save a life, and I race for the store entrance. The door opens again, and another man begins to exit, a gun in his hand. I step in front of him, aiming my weapon.

"FBI!" I shout, wholly concerned about what's in front of me and what could happen behind me, and I add, "Step back and drop the weapon, or I'll shoot."

As I've been trained, I document his appearance. Tall, fit, his jawline defined, his face chiseled, the slight lines at his eyes aging him to thirty, and despite his long blond hair tied at his nape, he reads military to me.

"Easy there," he says smoothly, seemingly unaffected by the fact that I could shoot him dead. But he smartly responds to the threat I represent, holding his hands and his weapon upright and taking several wide steps backward. "I'm not the bad guy here. I'm licensed to carry. I was here when the robbery took place. I tried to stop it."

I'm inside the door now, and there is a woman behind the counter, literally trembling, and another man on the ground, who appears to be knocked out. There's also a gun on the counter.

"It was his," the blond man says. "He was holding it on her, and I knocked him out."

"It's true," the woman argues in his defense. "This man just walked right up to the guy and knocked him out. His partner ran after that. I was so scared." Her voice trembles. "I thought I was going to die."

"You should cuff him," the blond stranger says. "He might not be out long."

"Drop the weapon," I demand again, my voice cool but sharp this time. "Then I'll cuff you both."

He flips his gun around, offering me the butt, his blue eyes alert but not challenging.

"That's not the ground," I warn.

"Yeah, well, your back is to the door, and both of us are thinking about what's behind you right now."

He's right.

I need to lock the door and reposition myself away from the entrance, but that's not an easy task with a rack of chips in the way, therefore I will not be doing so until his gun is on the ground.

"He helped me, miss!" the woman behind the counter shouts. "He saved my life. That man was going to shoot me."

This might be true, I think, but I've been trained to expect the worst. A trick is a trick. A spade is not always a spade. I don't look at her. I stay focused on the blue-eyed devil in front of me, and he *is* a devil until I know differently. "Drop the damn weapon and get on your knees!" I order. "Or I *will* shoot you."

He grimaces. "This is a mistake," he says, but he goes down on one knee and sets his gun in front of him, lifting his arms and lacing his fingers behind his head, as if this isn't his first rodeo. He's been in this position before now. I kick away his gun.

I'm about to lock the door before I cuff him and the man he knocked out, when it blasts open. My heart rate spikes and I quickly move to my power position, stepping behind the man now on his knee and pointing my weapon over his head at the door as yet another man, this one thankfully familiar, walks into the store. Tall, broad, muscled up with a salt and pepper goatee, my stepfather, Kurt, is holding a handgun with the ease of a practiced man who is, in fact, a legend with the military. Literally. Most people don't know if he's real or not.

"You're clear in the front," he announces, "and I called for backup."

Of course, he did. Kurt not only owns a sprawling property called "The Ranch" not far from here, he acts as if he owns the entire neighborhood. Not to mention the fact that everyone in law enforcement also knows him and for good reason. They all want to train with him, and few will ever earn that opportunity.

He glances at the man on his knees. "Lucifer," he says casually. "I didn't know you were back."

"It was past due," the man I now know to be called "Lucifer" replies. He's not the devil by name, but close enough. And it's a nickname that combined with his familiarity with my stepfather tells a story about who, and *what* kind of man, I have on his knees.

"He was walking around waving a gun," I say. "Who he is to you?"

"I was *not* waving a gun," Lucifer rebuts coolly. "I was aiming it at the guy who tried to kill the nice lady behind the counter."

"That's true!" the woman calls out, motioning to the guy on the floor. "This fool was pointing the gun at me, and Lucifer walked right up to him, and the next thing I knew, he just knocked him out."

Kurt's lips curve in amusement, and he casts me sideways look. "He's good, baby girl. One of my best, much like you. Let him up." He moves on as if his word is law, and not without history. Most people, me included, listen when he talks. Kurt trains government-employed killers. Obviously, Lucifer is one of the elite who have been privy to that training. In other words,

Lucifer is not "good," not in a literal sense, but he's also clearly not guilty of robbing the store.

"Have you cleared the rear of the store?" Kurt asks.

"No, not yet," I say. "I was dealing with your man who refused to drop his weapon."

"When have I ever taught you to drop your weapon, sweetie?" He winks. "Give him a break. I'll handle the rear." He steps around me and heads down an aisle.

Sirens shrill, growing closer.

I grimace at Lucifer, who's now shifted his position to look up at me with those damn bright blue eyes I notice *yet again*, and there's a quirk to his lips. He's amused. I am definitely not. He's also a little too good-looking for the safety of all of womankind. He arches a brow. "Can I retrieve my weapon and stand up?" he asks.

"We both know Kurt didn't teach you to ask."

"I usually don't."

"Then why are you now?"

"Respect."

"For Kurt, not me." I don't give him time to answer. "Get up. Wait outside and don't go anywhere. Law enforcement will want to interview you."

"Yes, ma'am," he says, retrieving his weapon as he stands and slides it into a holster under his leather jacket.

"All clear!" Kurt calls out. "We have a scared young man here in the freezer area. Rear door is locked."

"That's Jonathan!" the woman behind the counter shouts. "Poor Jonathan." The woman rounds the counter and rushes toward Kurt and the other man.

Lucifer steps closer, towering over me, and while some might think this move would intimidate me, Lucifer knows Kurt trained me, therefore, he already knows that won't work on me.

As if confirming that truth, he says, "I heard Kurt had a badass daughter. I had no idea she would one day be the woman who brought me to my knees quite literally."

He may, or may not, be flirting with me. "Kurt teaches us to resist. I'm surprised you even got on your knees."

"Sometimes, a man doesn't want to resist."

He *is* flirting.

And I'm not nearly immune as I should be, either.

A police officer steps inside the store and we both glance that direction. The officer stomps a path toward us. Lucifer's eyes return to me, potent in their impact. "I'll see you outside, *Ana*," he says, making it clear that he knows my name, through my association with Kurt. "And just for the record," he adds. "My name is Luke Remington though I was born Lucas, and became Luke, per my mother, when I insisted on that change at age five. I also answer to Lucifer, my code name when I was flying jets. It has nothing to do with any work I did for, or with, Kurt. I'm not one of Kurt's men, nor have I ever been one of his men." He walks toward the officer, and I'm officially intrigued by this stranger who has an association I avoid: that being Kurt. No one who knows Kurt denies his influence and catches my attention. And yet, Lucifer, *Luke,* Lucas, whatever you want to call him, just did.

***

It's a good hour later when I step outside the store into a cold, but not brutally cold, night to find Luke under a streetlight, leaning on a motorcycle seat, booted ankles crossed while talking with Kurt. Kurt pats his shoulder and then heads for his pickup truck. Luke doesn't move. His eyes are on me. He's waiting *on me.* There are butterflies in my belly that defy my badass reputation he's claimed I own. I don't know what is going on with me and this man, but I'm not interested in finding out, I tell myself, but my feet are still moving in his direction.

He watches me the entire walk, hyper-focused on me, and just me, and I don't look away. A badass chick would never look away. I stop in front of him, a little too close I decide when he pushes off the bike and straightens, eating up the space between us. Now we're so close that I can feel his body heat. I wonder if he can feel mine. Of course, he can, can't he?

"I thought maybe I could take you for a coffee to apologize for that incident inside," he suggests.

"You were a hero," I say. "No need to apologize for that."

His eyes twinkle with mischief. "And you're not going to apologize for putting me on my knees, now are you?"

"No," I say. "No, I am not. I was doing my job but I still concede that you were ultimately a hero."

The mischief fades from his voice, his tone flat now. "I'm no hero, I just happened to be here. How about that coffee?"

My answer is no answer at all. It's also not a question. "You trained with Kurt."

"That did happen," he confirms.

"Then you're one of his, and I don't do coffee with his men."

"I'm not one of his."

"Okay," I say, not about to argue this point. Obviously, there's something I don't know. "Thank you for saving those people's lives tonight. And if you're going to be around, I'll see you again, I'm certain."

"Okay then," he says, with a slight lean of his chin. "I respect your rules but I still want you to know that I've had a really shitty couple of days, and somehow the idea of taking you to coffee and kissing you after made this day worth living."

I blink in surprise, and as Kurt's stepdaughter, I'm rarely surprised. My heart punches at my chest. "You don't even know me."

"Is that still a no to the coffee?"

"No coffee," I say, feeling my limbs grow heavy and warm. "Goodnight, Luke."

I turn and start walking, and I don't know why but after a few steps in, I stop and turn to face him. "Why was it a shitty few days?"

"My last week of enlistment, my last day of service, and one of my closest friends was killed in action. Made me wonder why the fuck I stayed in so long."

I suck in a breath. He lost a friend and he still saved two lives tonight. And now, he says taking me to coffee and kissing me would make this day worth living? I close the space between us, about to break every rule I've ever made about all things Kurt. "Yes to coffee. No to the kiss. I'll take my own car. Brewster's is one block down on the right."

His lips curve. "All right then. Brewster's it is. And I can accept the kiss is off the table. *For now.*"

For now. God, why do I like that response so much? I turn and start walking toward my car with the roaring feeling that this decision will change my life, which is silly. It's just coffee.

CHAPTER TWO

Lucifer

SIX YEARS LATER...

"Tell me again, why the hell am I on a damn horse, riding it in the middle of hellfire heat?" Adam and Savage, two of my cohorts from Walker Security, our employer, flank me left and right, but it's Adam I'm glaring at now. "I wouldn't have saved your life down on the border six months ago if I knew you'd drag me back into the hellfire on horseback."

He laughs. "It's Texas, and it's not that bad. The food is good and the women are hotter than the sun."

"And the mosquitos are the size of small birds," I grumble, smacking at one on my arm.

"Training, man," he says. "Bossman Blake wants us to be versatile."

Walker Security is an elite worldwide operation, offering a broad range of private hire security, but they also run security for most of the airports, and consult with almost every facet of law enforcement. I came to them well-trained, but in a year and half, I've learned you're never well trained enough to suit the Walker operation.

I snort. "You never know when we might need to escape by horseback despite living in New York City." Of course, we're rarely in New York City. We're all over the world, where I hope like fuck I will never have to count on a horse to escape trouble.

Savage, the general troublemaker of our group, chimes in with, "What he's trying to tell you there, cowboy, is that *asses* need to know how to ride *asses*."

"Says the biggest ass I know," I reply because everyone knows that comment resembles Savage. Savage, like Adam, is tall, broad, and wears his dark hair military-style. However, Savage, unlike Adam, is tatted up, with a big-ass scar down his cheek, which he probably got from being a dick to someone with less patience than me.

"If it looks like an ass," Adam says, "and acts like an ass, he is an ass."

I'm not sure which one of us he's talking about or if it's both, but Savage assumes the retort to be directed toward him. "Shut the fuck up," he grumbles, and in true fashion to his usual stupid jokes, he adds, "Adam minus his Eve makes for a man with nothing better to do than talk about asses."

My cellphone buzzes and I grab it from my pocket, eyeing the text that reads: *Luc, man, we need to talk. Call me. Sooner than later. It's life or death.*

This is coming from a voice from my past, and when this voice speaks, you take him seriously. I've officially had enough horseback riding for one day. While me and my tats and unruly blond hair might not look the part, I did plenty of cowboying in my youth. Enough to last a lifetime, actually. I give Melvin, my horse, a nudge and head for the stables. By the time I'm dismounting, Adam and Savage are headed my way and closing in fast. While the Walker team has been good to me, they're as sticky as a bottle of Gorilla glue.

I offer my reins to the awaiting ranch hand eager to claim my ride and give Melvin a short thank-you pet. He's a fine boy. It's not his fault this place reminds me of a long time ago, better kept in the past. Eager to make this call on my own, I start walking before I end up with company. Adam, an ex-SEAL Team Six member who's a good guy, a better man than me, and still thinks I'm not worthy of my nickname, Lucifer, a label he believes I got for my crazy stunts flying fighter jets.

He's wrong. So is anyone else who believes that bullshit.

But I'd rather keep them keeping on believing.

I am not the blond-haired, blue-eyed angel my mother believed she brought into this world, and some who know me from another life would say that's never going to change.

At this point, I'm already straddling the motorcycle I rode into this place on, trying to get some space to make this call. I pass by the ranch house and head toward the main road. When I'm almost to the highway, I pull off under a thicket of trees. Once I'm off my bike and leaning on a willow tree, I pull my phone out and dial Jake, someone who really does know the meaning of hell because he visited it with me.

I punch in his number, and when it rings, I expect him to answer right away. It goes to voicemail. My brows dip, an uneasy feeling sliding over me. I try again with the same results. I text him: *I'm trying to call. What's up?* I wait a few seconds, which turns into a full minute and nothing. No reply. That uneasy feeling expands. Engines roar, and I glance up to find Adam and Savage speeding my way. Son of a bitch, they really do stick like damn glue. I shoot off another text and shove my phone into my pocket. At this point, Adam and Savage have already dismounted and are up close in my personal space.

Savage grabs his inner thighs. "I feel like I've been violated."

"Try moving with the horse, not against the horse, like you would your woman," I say, straddling my bike. "Like this," I add, revving my engine, and getting the fuck out of there.

They're going to follow me, but I'm not stopping until the time is right. That time is about ten minutes later when I dismount in front of Whataburger. I'm already at the counter when Adam steps to my side—just Adam, which means he wants to have a serious one-on-one. I expected as much. I hand him a cup. "I ordered for you."

"How'd you know Savage wasn't coming?"

"Because I know you," I say, walking to the ice machine and filling my cup. Adam does the same, but as expected, he doesn't start asking questions just yet.

We sit down, and I say, "I love this place."

"Yeah," Adam says. "Me too. You going to tell me what's going on?"

"Not until I eat this burger."

He just looks at me, and I know he'll just keep on staring at me if I don't talk while I eat. He has to do me like that. "You really know how to ruin a hot burger."

"I'll buy you another."

"You don't have to. There's no story here. An old friend texted me with an urgent message. He's not taking my calls or texts now."

"The kind of old friend none of us want to hear from." It's not a question.

"Yup," I say, unwrapping my burger and taking a bite of heaven. "Damn. This place is the best part of Texas."

"How much trouble is this, potentially?" Adam asks.

I don't bullshit Adam. He's too good a guy to deserve that shit. "The kind that makes you think you better savor your Whataburger with a chocolate shake because it might be your last meal." I grab my drink and sip the sweet beverage.

Adam grabs his drink and says, "Shit," before he sips as well.

That's right, I think—triple shit. My cellphone rings, and I grab it from the table, glance at the number, and give Adam a nod. It's him. I answer the line. "What the hell is going on, Jake?"

He's breathing hard. "A team of operatives just tried to take me the fuck out. I'm on foot in the damn woods."

I sit up straighter. "Who?"

"They found me. Fuck. I have to go. There's a hitlist, Luke. Son of a bitch." Gunfire sounds, and there's a bunch of shuffling sounds on his end.

I stand up. "Jake?"

There's more shuffling, the sound of Jake saying, "Eat shit, you bastard."

A man laughs and then a bullet sounds. I squeeze my eyes shut before I hear an unfamiliar voice say, "Hello, Luke. I bet I get to her before you do."

My heart stops beating for a moment. "If you touch her, you're dead."

He laughs. "We'll see." He hangs up.

I'm seeing red as I start walking toward the door, and contrary to the norm for me, I'm freaking the hell out. I'm outside, helmet in hand, when Adam steps to my side. "Where are we going?"

"Not we. Me. I'm off the books for at least a week."

"Like I said, where are we going?"

I could fight with him, but based on what I just overheard, backup might not be a bad idea. "Colorado, to save the only woman I ever loved. And we might need Savage's surgical skills. The last time I saw her, she shot me."

LISA RENEE JONES

CHAPTER THREE

Lucifer

Before Adam and I ever leave Whataburger, I dial Ana. I'm not surprised when she doesn't answer, but I try again. I call her ten freaking times and leave just as many messages.

"Jake is dead," I finally say to her machine. "I heard him die on the phone, while he warned me that we are next. I talked to his killer. He picked up the phone and challenged me to get to you first. He's coming for you, Ana, and I don't know who he is. This isn't a drill," I add, using the words her training tells her means business. I have to hope like hell that's enough.

I'm back at the ranch house, packing my bag when Luke Walker, the middle of the three founding Walker Security brothers, steps into the room I've been staying in at Cowboy's Family Ranch. And like all the brothers, his hair is dark, his build is fit, and his skills just as dangerous. I like Luke. He personifies his biblical name: a peacekeeper, a man of honor. There's a reason I never use Luke myself. I'm none of those things.

"Adam told me what's going on," he says. "I chartered you a plane to Colorado minus the pilot. That will have to be you."

I zip up my bag. "Thanks, man. I'm not turning that down." I take a step toward the door, ready to leave.

He doesn't budge. He's still blocking my exit. "The question is," he says, "how concerned should I be about three of my men, you included, visiting the woman that tried to kill you?"

I grimace and silently curse Adam for running his mouth. "I'm not taking Savage for wit," I say, "but ultimately, the only person she wants dead is me. She's FBI. She doesn't kill anyone she doesn't think deserves it."

His brow shoots up. "But she *did* try to kill you?"

"That's right," I say, offering no details, and I never will. Ever.

Luke is smart enough not to push, shifting to the next obvious question. "Who wants *her* dead?"

"I don't know."

"Do you know why?"

"As I said, she's an FBI agent. She has enemies."

"And yet, they seem to be using her as bait to get to *you.*"

"So it seems," I say dryly.

"Is that all you're going to tell me?"

"Yep," I say, and I don't apologize, either. My past is ugly, but it's buried well enough that not even Walker Security will uncover just how ugly. Unfortunately for Ana, that past is also her past.

He studies me a moment that turns into two, time I don't have right now, before he says, "Who was Jake?"

"Her godfather," I say.

"And her father?"

"Her father was a solider who died in a training accident when she was four. Jake was connected to Kurt, her stepfather, who raised her. Kurt's been dead for three years."

"Is this problem right now related to his death?"

More like his life, I think, but what I say is, "I don't know."

"And this hitlist Adam told me about?"

"If Jake said it exists, it exists. That's all I know right now."

"All right, then. You can't find out more information to tell me while you're flying a plane, and we all need to know more. I'll have Blake hack the dark web for answers."

Blake being his younger brother, is a world-class hacker. If anyone can get me that hitlist, it's him. I give Luke a nod of thanks, and he adds, "We have two men in Colorado free. What I need to know is how do you want to use them?"

"Depends on who they are."

"Hunter and Dexter."

Both are skilled, but I don't know them well enough to trust them. Adam, Savage, and the Walker brothers, I trust, and that says a lot coming from me. The rest of the bunch, I'm not even trying to trust them.

"Find her," I say. "And then stand down. She's highly skilled, more so than they'll expect from her badge."

"Obviously," he says. "She managed to shoot you."

"I didn't exactly see it coming," I rebut.

"Obviously," he says again. "I assume she won't take your calls to accept their help?"

"Funny thing," I say with a bitter laugh. "Once a woman hates you enough to shoot you, she doesn't take too kindly to you calling her. I left her messages."

I expect him to keep pushing, to ask a question I won't answer, but all he says is, "Then you better get moving." He steps into the hallway to give me room to exit.

I shift the bag to my shoulder and exit the room, pausing next to Luke. "Thank you, Luke."

He pats my shoulder. "You're family now, man. This is what we do. Next time, come to me."

Family. I never thought that word and me would ever be spoken in the same sentence again, but hell, maybe. I'd die for any of these guys. The problem is that doesn't always matter. I learned that the hard way.

I give him another nod, but I'm not sure there will be a next time. While it's true I was in a different job and a different place in life, firm in my own ideals, before I joined Walker, I'm not a different person. The man who wanted to blow up the world and go up in flames still wants to blow up the world and go up in flames. And if that dickhead on the phone kills Ana, I will. After I kill him, brutally and painfully.

CHAPTER FOUR

Lucifer

By the time I'm doing a safety check on the jet, I'll be flying to Colorado, I've heard nothing good. Ana hasn't called me back. Blake can't find anything worth knowing on the dark web. Our boots on the ground in Colorado can't get eyes on Ana. They've even gone so far as to confirm she's not at the FBI offices. By the time we're wheels off the tarmac, Blake is trying to use her cellphone to ping her location, and I've left her partner, "Darius the Dickhead," a message, telling him she's in danger, which means he could be, too. In other words, my progress on saving Ana sucks.

Worse, the damn plane doesn't have internet.

I spend three hours in that plane, that should have been two, after a shit ton of turbulence forces me to take a detour from hell before we finally touch down in Centennial, Colorado, just outside Denver. My cell rings almost instantly, and while I'm looking for a call from Ana, or even Darius, it's Blake. "Yeah, man," I answer.

"Her phone's not pinging. I'm guessing it's off. I'm going through the security footage to try and figure out when she was last at her office and how she left to put the traffic cameras to use. More soon."

We disconnect, then I dial Darius, who once again doesn't answer my call, which could be because he's undercover, or it could simply be the fact that he hates me almost as much as Ana does. I can't get off this damn plane fast enough. "How are we riding out of here?" I ask Adam, who's still sitting shotgun.

"Riding dirty in a basic black sedan, man. Luke arranged it. We're set."

Fuck yes, I think. "Let's roll then."

A few minutes later, I'm finally in the backseat of the car with Savage at the wheel and Adam riding shotgun—only we're not moving. We're wasting valuable time, sitting on the tarmac with Savage waiting on me to tell him where to go. I punch in Darius' number again, and thank fuck, he picks up. "I'm not getting in between you and Ana. That ship has sailed."

"Where is she?"

"She's not my partner anymore. And I don't know where she is. I'm telling you, man—"

In other words, he knows. "Call her. Tell her—"

"No," he says. "*Fuck no*. I'm not getting involved. Let me drink my beer and eat my pizza. I only answered to say no." He hangs up.

I curse and ball my fist. "Idiot," I murmur, thinking he too could be on the hitlist, and Ana will never forgive me if he ends up dead. I text him: *Listen to the message I left you, dickhead,* before I tap Savage's seat and say, "Drive," praying I'm not too late to save Ana. And her dipshit partner, who claims to be her ex-partner.

CHAPTER FIVE

Lucifer

Darius is not going to open his door for me, of that, I'm sure.

Therefore, thirty minutes after that call where he hung up on me, we roll into Littleton, where he lives, which is basically just one of the many extensions of Denver. We have a plan in play. Adam, Mr. Master of Disguise, The Invisible Man when he wants to be, despite being six-foot-four and you'd think hard to miss, is our key player. He'll pretend to be a food delivery guy at the wrong house. Savage is presently in the bushes near the porch. I'm on the right side of the house. Adam pulls the sedan into the driveway, climbs out, his baseball hat backward and a McDonald's bag in his hand, compliments of a drive-thru as he heads for the front door.

Since I've been here before, and I know the lay of the land, this is my cue to head to the rear of the house with the intent to enter through the back door while Darius is dealing with a seemingly confused Adam. Since Darius is Mr. Bad Ass FBI agent and doesn't think he needs a security system—which is the dumbest thing I've ever heard, considering how many people he pisses off—breaking into his house should be the easiest part of this encounter. Once I've opened the screen door, I use a hand tool I carry with me, and bingo, the door is open. I slide it to the left and at the sound of an obvious scuffle going on inside, I tense. Damn it, I can't be too late to save her. I refuse to accept that answer, but it makes sense that I'm not the only one thinking Ana's partner, or ex-partner, or whatever the fuck he is, is the way to find her.

With my gun drawn, I charge through the kitchen and clear the doorway, adrenaline spiking with the sight before me. Ana is here, her long blonde hair tied at her nape, sitting on top of Adam, her gun pointed at his face.

Meanwhile, Savage has Darius on the ground, his foot on his chest, his gun pointed at his head. "You shoot, sweetheart," Savage warns Ana, "I promise you, Darius won't walk out of here alive."

Ana's green eyes meet mine, cutting and angry, and yet there is a charge in the air between us that is everything and somehow not a damn thing.

"*You*," she hisses, her shock making it clear that she has not heard any of my messages. "What do you want?"

"Well, for starters, and even though seeing you straddle another man makes me want to shoot him more than you do, I'd rather you not. He's here to help me save your life."

CHAPTER SIX

Lucifer

"Saving my life was never what you were good at, Lucifer," Ana says.

I flinch with that name on her tongue and all the reasons it became who I am to her. And she's still straddling Adam, damn it, right across his hips. "Get off of him," I order softly.

"That's your brilliant plan?" Adam challenges, and while I can't see his eyes and his intent, his fingers flex by his side, ready to move. "Handle her, or I will."

"*You'll* handle me?" Ana asks, laughing. "I have the gun, and I know how to handle it and you a whole lot better than you think I do."

"I'm aware of your skills and your anger issues, sweetheart," Adam replies. "And we both know I'm the wrong guy. You and Lucifer need to deal with your dirty laundry and do it now because some worse shit is headed our way any minute."

The exchange is an opportunity I put to good use. Just that quick, I'm in front of her, eye to eye with the woman I loved and lost, kneeling at the top of Adam's head. And she does exactly what I expect her to, shifting her weapon to target me instead. "Do not even think about getting closer."

At this point, size matters, even if Ana doesn't want to admit it. Adam is huge, and she is petite. He could overpower her and escape, but he doesn't move. He's waiting on the right moment, which Darius creates as he shouts, "I'm going to kill you, Lucifer, you bastard. You *are* the devil."

"You assume I'm going to let you live to try," Savage snaps.

Adam moves then and has her gun in a flash, but Ana is well trained and reacts smartly, quickly. Instantly, I'm standing, and so is she, and she's holding yet another gun she's pulled from her person at my chest. "I'll kill him!" she shouts at the room while her eyes burn into mine. "You must have a death wish. I can't believe you came back here."

Her anger, her contempt, and the burn of her believing the worst of me is a fresh blade in my heart, but it also pisses me the fuck off. "Kasey tried to kill me, Ana," I say softly, for her ears only. "I had to kill him."

"He wouldn't—"

"He did," I snap. "He was dirty."

Her jaw clenches. "He wasn't dirty."

"Some part of you knows the truth. You just wish it were the other way around, that I'm dead and he's not. Shoot me, Ana. If that's what will make you happy, fucking shoot me again."

"God, you really are the devil. Don't tempt me, Lucifer." Her hand trembles, when it never trembles, and her energy radiates with anger and emotion. "Don't tempt me," she repeats in a raspy hiss.

Suddenly Savage is beside us, and he grabs the gun, yanking it away from Ana. "No one in this room is shooting anyone except maybe Darius the Dickhead, who irritates the fuck out of me. This is why Adam is currently tying his ass up. He's safer that way." He glowers at me. "I can't save you if I let her shoot you at this close range. And you can't save her if you're dead." He glances at her and shoves her gun in his pants. "He's a good guy. Whoever the fuck Kasey is, he shot him because he deserved it."

She rotates on Savage and smacks him in the face. "Fuck," he snaps. "That wasn't nice."

"He was my brother, you asshole. And if I shoot Lucifer again, I don't intend for anyone to save him."

Savage gapes at me. "You killed *her brother*? Fuck, man, there's no coming back from that."

Aware of that truth, and even more so the fact that we could be attacked at any moment, I grab Ana. She slaps me hard in the face, yet the sting doesn't stop me from throwing her over my shoulder. She tries to kick and fight, of course, and she calls me names, but Adam was right. This is between me and her, *just* me and her, which is why I walk toward the location I know to be a bedroom.

Once we're inside, I kick the door shut and set her down.

Now we're alone, and I'm not at all surprised when she slaps me again. And again. I let her just do it. Maybe I want the pain. Maybe I deserve the pain, but it can't hurt as much as the day she told me she hated me. The day she tried to kill me and almost succeeded.

"Do something!" she shouts at me. "Stop just standing there."

I catch her arms and drag her to me, turning her and pinning her between me and the door. "Does that work?"

CHAPTER SEVEN

Lucifer

Ana doesn't jerk at her hands or fight me. She's trained not to waste energy she can't afford to expel. Her eyes meet mine, and there is a punch of history between us. Four years of history that started in a corner store turned into an engagement ring, and then ended with a bullet in my gut. I never thought I'd be this close to her again, even if I had to pin her to a door to make it happen. She's still beautiful. She still smells delicious. And I still fucking love her, and I hate that I do.

She feels all the things I do. I see the flare of memories in her eyes, and I damn sure feel the push and pull between us that is familiar, ripe with history, and burning with the knowledge that we are still wickedly hot together. I know the exact moment she realizes this, the moment she hates me for it, the moment she really does want to shoot me all over again.

"Why are you not in hell already, Lucifer?" she demands softly.

I'd flinch, but she'd enjoy it too much, and of all the ways I'm willing to offer her pleasure, that's not the kind of pleasure I intend to give Ana now or later.

"Because, apparently," I say, "I was supposed to stick around to keep you alive so you could have another shot at me, Ana, but do it later. Jake's dead."

She blanches. "What?"

"He called me to warn me about a hitlist. He was being chased." My lips thin. "I heard him die, and then a

29

man came on the line. He told me you were next and challenged me to get to you first. I was in Texas, and you wouldn't take my calls."

"I was undercover. Darius grabbed my phone by accident. That's why I'm here."

In other words, Darius knew I was calling her. He might have even read the text message, but for now, I leave that alone. "Bottom line, Ana, it's been hours since that threat was issued and that's too long for us to be in a place where you're easily located."

Her lashes lower, her expression rippling with tension, before she looks at me again. "Let me go. *Please*."

"Are you going to hit me again?"

"Not now. I make no promises about later."

The fact that she suggests there will be a later at all is enough for me. I ease my grip on her wrists and reluctantly lift my body from hers. She doesn't move, she doesn't run, but then it's not Ana's nature to run at all.

"Do you know what this is about? And why it's happening now?"

"Other than the obvious connection to the past, none. You know I left my team behind when—" I stop myself before I say, "when your brother died" and decide on, "a long time ago."

"You have to have some idea what this is about, Luke."

Luke.

Not Lucifer.

That little change is not little at all, but the minute I tell her where this threat originates, she'll be back to Lucifer. But I also have no choice. "I told you—"

She points her finger at me. "Do not tell me my brother was dirty. Do *not*. He was not dirty." She steps around me now and walks away, but I don't immediately turn and not because I trust her not to shoot me. She still might. And fuck me, if she does, so be it.

Weary as fuck, I pant out a breath, run a hand through my hair, and turn to face her, hands settling on my hips under the puffer jacket someone shoved at me when we exited the plane earlier. "We need to leave."

"We don't need to do anything."

"Whoever this is, used you as bait. I'm not leaving you behind."

"You know I can handle myself."

"Yes. I have the scar from the bullet hole to show for it, too, but this is bigger than either of us. And thank fuck you don't have a gun right now because I'm just going to put this out there: considering the challenge I was issued, it seems to me the man who issued it knew I wasn't going to be able to call you and warn you when he hung up. In other words, this rings of someone close to you being involved."

"Are you suggesting that someone is Darius?"

I narrow my eyes at her. "Are *you*?"

"I don't trust anyone anymore."

"Right," I say dryly. "Thanks to me. We need to get the fuck out of here."

No sooner have I said those words than gunfire erupts in the front of the house.

CHAPTER EIGHT

Ana

My world is already spinning with Luke's return, even before the sound of bullets rings out in front of Darius's house. Imminent danger tells me it's time to find my dark zone, that place in my mind Kurt trained me to find in battle, a place where there are no emotions, only skills. If only it were that easy with Luke standing in front of me again.

"There's a window off the side of the house downstairs," I say, moving toward him and the door. "Exit to the hallway and cut left. And your men better not leave Darius in a damn closet, or I swear to you—"

"They won't leave him," he says, "but I swear to *you*, if I find out he sold you out tonight, he's going to wish he was in the closet." He reaches under his pant leg and produces a Glock, offering it to me. "Don't shoot me. I'm the one trying to save your life."

My stomach knots with the idea of that bullet I put in his belly. I was angry. I was hurt. Things happened that were not supposed to happen. All sourced from the fact that I was scared I was too in love with him to see him coming for me next. Now, years later, especially with him standing right here in front of me again, I don't know what I feel anymore. I snatch the weapon from him. "Open the door."

He pulls another weapon from behind his back in his belt, which tells me he could have used it on me earlier in the living room, yet he didn't. I don't allow myself to start thinking about what that means. Dark means dark, no emotions.

Luke opens the door, and the sound of gunfire exchange remains in the front of the house.

He grabs me and pulls me in front of him, and even now, in supposed dark mode, fighting for my life, his touch burns through me. So does his intent of ensuring that any bullets coming from the front of the house hit him first, but I remind myself that his love for me was always the definition of a scam. Focusing on freedom from the gunfire, I move down the hallway, find the door I'm looking for, and rush down the stairwell to the lower level. Luke is right behind me, and while there is a lock on the door, he doesn't use it, leaving his men and Darius a way to escape. It also offers the enemy the ability to follow us, but I'd have done the same thing. Everything he does is what I would do—it always was, until it wasn't.

Until he killed my brother.

Anger burns in my belly, and I cross the entertainment area of the house and head straight for a window that is high above my head. I look around for something to stand on, but Luke is already right beside me. He catches me to him and turns me, my body folded against his big, powerful one, and before I know his intent, he's tangled fingers in my hair. "In case I don't get out of here alive and you do," he says, and then his mouth is slanting over my mouth.

I moan with the familiar, long-lost taste of him on my lips. I don't mean to, I really don't, but when his tongue finds my tongue, and sensations burn through me, I am his again. I am living a million delicious moments with this man. My arms slide around him, and I am back in time, replaying the night we met. Back in the parking lot of Brewster's coffee house. We'd spent two hours talking, and when he'd walked me to my car, we'd stood there staring at each other.

"I have to do it," he'd said, and then he'd moved.

A moment later, he'd kissed me, and it wasn't a tentative, gentle kiss. He'd molded my hips to his hips and claimed my mouth with a possessive slide of his tongue, in a sultry way that had left me helpless to resist. The world had faded and all there was, was this man boldly kissing me when no one else in Kurt's world would dare such a thing. The memory consumes me, the way Luke always consumes me, from the instant I met him. I sink into the here and now, into the kiss I never thought I'd know again, drinking him in and melting with the wicked wild way this man undoes me.

Until gunfire just above the stairway jolts us apart.

"That meant nothing," I whisper.

"It means I can die a happy man, sweetheart, but I'd rather not. Let's get the fuck out of here." He turns me and lifts me toward the window. I shove my gun in my belt, and I'm already reaching for the lock when Luke moans, "God, woman, you still have a fine as fuck ass."

"Stop looking at my ass," I snap, working the lock and shoving the window open, but I'm still aware of the taste of him on my lips, and of every burning second his hands are on my body.

The minute the window is open, he hikes me upward, and I rest my gun just outside on the ground, eyeing left and right, but the bushes block my view. They also offer me coverage. "Clear," I whisper, and he and I both lift me forward. Once I'm outside, gun in hand, in a squatting position, I have a decision to make. Any second now, Luke will join me, and then I'm riding this ride with him. Do I trust him that much? I just kissed the man. I obviously *want* to trust him that much, but he killed my brother. He deserves my bullet, and nothing more.

Still, damn him. Hesitation burns my feet to the ground, the part of me that never let him go, not wanting to again, but this is about survival. *Dark mode, Ana,* I can hear Kurt say in my head. Luke appears in the window, and I look right and start moving. I don't want to desert Darius, but he's been off lately, and something in my gut tells me Luke isn't wrong to suspect him.

"Damn it, Ana," I hear Luke curse, but I don't look back. He's not Luke. He's *Lucifer,* and I'd do well to remember that. I round the bushes and take off on a run, leaving the devil who killed my brother behind. This time, for good.

CHAPTER NINE

Ava

THE PAST...

A loud banging has me jolting into a sitting position on my bed, darkness suffocating me, and my heart thundering in my chest. My fingers curl on the edge of the mattress, but otherwise, I don't dare move, listening for another sound. Not sure if the banging was even real or another one of the nightmares that have haunted me this past year.

Seconds tick by and there is nothing, not even a tick of a clock, when suddenly, a flashlight shines in my eyes. "Up, little girl," my stepfather says. "You have five minutes to be dressed and outside."

Objection and relief rush over me all at once. "It's still dark, and I'm tired."

"Exactly the point. No one attacks you when it's convenient. "

"I'm fourteen, Kurt," I say, calling him by his name. He never wanted to be "Dad" anyway. He said that's fake imagery and I don't need a sense of reality that isn't real.

He kneels in front of me and shines the light on both our faces. "I wish like hell that mattered. And I wish like hell your mother wasn't gone, but she is. Now that your brother is off serving his country, we're all we have, you and me."

"I miss my mom," I whisper.

"I know you do," he says. "But feeling sorry for yourself gets you nowhere. And one day, you'll understand that. Just like one day, they will come for you to get to me. You have to be their worst nightmare."

"Why now? Why must I train now? You never made me before."

"That was a mistake. We learn from our mistakes."

"Send me away."

"They'll find you, Ana."

"Who?" I demand, my voice lifting. "Who will find me?"

"My enemies. Do you want to live or die?"

Tears burn in my eyes. "Live."

"Then let's go."

"Where?"

"Into the woods." He stands up and flips off the light, and I can tell he's leaving.

"Did Mom really die in a car accident?" I call out urgently.

He's silent a moment and then, "No."

My heart is racing again. "Did they kill her?"

"Yes."

"Did you kill them?"

"Yes, but there is always another enemy. No more fear, baby. No more."

The door opens and shuts, and tears stream down my cheeks with his confession. Mom didn't die in a car accident. I'm glad he killed them. I wish I could have killed them. I stand up. No more fear.

CHAPTER TEN

Ana

Darius lives on three acres in an area of Littleton that borders a heavily retailed section of the city, but nevertheless, the houses are more rural. This means my escape goal must include protecting those nearby homeowners. With that in mind, I don't travel left or right or even forward toward the nearest homes, but rather back and down, into the woods. It's far from the easiest path in what is now the dark of night, but as I start the treacherous hike, not for the first time, I'm thankful Kurt treated me like a soldier in training all of those years.

Not daring to use the flashlight I carry in my pocket, moonlight is both my friend and enemy as it guides my path, but in doing so, also limits my coverage. The sooner I'm deeper into the onset of trees, the better, and in an effort to achieve said goal quickly, I cover my eyes with my arm and push myself forward, charging through the foliage. As branches and the cold night bite at my body, I thank God I'm in thick jeans and boots. A coat would be a plus. I simply don't have one. About a third of the way into my travels, I pause, squat down, and listen.

Seconds tick by, and I hear nothing but nature, crickets chirping and an owl hooting. Moving again, I maneuver through a darkening path for another mile or so before I cut left toward an attendant-free gas station

I've been to with Darius. Of course, I was smart enough to travel there by car, not on foot like last time, but at least I have an idea of where the woods open to its location. Once I'm on the outskirts of the parking lot, still sheltered by the woods, I scan the area to find no one present.

My next move will be risky and must be strategic.

On the other side of the station is a shopping center that is deserted at this time of night. In other words, I'd be easy to spot, though there would be nooks and crannies in store entrances worthy of consideration. For now, I need to get to the opposite side of that station, hidden by the building, where I can decide the best coverage move. It's not a far run, but to get there from here, I'm still forced to expose myself, and I can almost hear my stepfather saying, "be invisible, not stupid." *Sometimes invisible isn't possible*, I think—a tic forming in my jaw. Unless Luke and his men killed the enemies, one of those enemies is coming after me in the woods. The longer I sit here, the longer I give them to catch up to my position.

I spend about three minutes listening for any signs of trouble, then I draw my weapon from the holster under my jacket and take off running. My heart races, my body pumps, and when I round the corner of the store, I think I'm safe, only to have a man in all black, including the ski mask covering his face, point a gun at me. But I'm also pointing my gun at him. It's not my first stand-off, and I'm confident I'll win this confrontation until I feel the energy shift at my back and know someone is behind me. I'm going to die, and all I can think is that kissing Luke wasn't such a mistake, after all.

The very next moment after that thought, there is a gunshot at my back. I sense the man in front of me is going to shoot me, so I shoot him first. I whirl around to find another man on the ground and Luke right beside me. "You're welcome," he says, and before I know it, he's strapping a zip tie to my arm and his own. "You aren't getting away again. You almost died."

I jerk at our connected wrists. "Get this off. We need our hands free to shoot."

"I shoot with both hands, sweetheart. You know that." He steps into me, his hand and gun at my hip, and says, "I left you your right arm, and your weapon in your hand, sweetheart, so either shoot me or let's move."

CHAPTER ELEVEN

Ana

Luke laces the fingers of our connected wrists. "What are we doing, sweetheart?"

Sweetheart.

The familiar endearment I haven't heard from him in years, and thought I'd never hear again, sideswipes me with an emotional undoing. My stomach is fluttering like I'm a silly schoolgirl who has my crush standing in front of me, not the FBI agent I am, who's presently cuffed to my ex while two dead bodies lie at my feet. The ex who took what was precious to me. What kind of sick person am I to still want him?

"He was my brother," I whisper.

"And there's not a day of my life that doesn't eat me alive, Ana," he promises, "but we *can't* do this right now. We don't have that time. Make a decision. Shoot me and run without me, or don't, and let's get the hell out of here."

I'm not going to shoot him, and he knows it. The night he ended up with a bullet in his gut was complicated, and I was shredded with grief, trembling all over, angry, scared, and careless, when I'm never careless. But as he said, now is not the time, so I simply say, "What's the plan?"

Relief washes over his chiseled features, and then, with the gun in his hand, he cups my head and kisses me hard and fast on the mouth. "I might not be able to make you love me again, but I'm going to make you want me."

"Damn you, Lucifer," I say because right now, he really is the devil.

"Damn me later. I have things to do right now, and so do you." He's already pulling me with him to ease around the corner. "Clear," he says, motioning to the other side of the building as he drags me along with him.

I want to tell him to uncuff me, but I know this man more than I know any other on this planet—or so I once thought—and it's wasted breath. He made a decision. He's sticking with it, with stubborn insistence, beyond what is even reasonable. For now, I follow him around like a puppet, trying to help us clear our path when I'd do a much better job with my arm free.

Once we're certain no one is coming at our back, he leads me toward the shopping center. I don't tell him it's risky. One thing I know about this man is that he knows how to stay alive. *To the demise of my brother*, I think bitterly, but I shove away the thought. We're on the same team right now, fighting the same enemy, and the truth is that if Darius is involved—which I pray he isn't—who else might be as well? I'm no fool. Judging from Luke's earlier company, and as expected, he's surrounded with talent, and Luke himself, has resources that I alone do not. Not when I don't know who to trust.

At this point, we've cleared the gas station parking lot and are climbing a grassy incline, and I, for one, do so, thankful it's without a blast of bullets at our back. We round the top, and I dig in my heels and jerk against Luke's arm at the sight of a vehicle. "Luke."

"It's ours," he says, already pulling me forward toward a black sedan, and soon the hill becomes our bulletproof wall. I should be relieved, however, it's also the perfect place to be picked off from the top.

Seemingly cognizant of that fact, Luke clicks the locks on the vehicle and unlocks it before we're even there. Relief finally washes over me as he opens the door, and I slide in, unable to go far with our connected arms.

He joins me and shuts us inside, our legs pressed intimately together even as he uses both of our hands to turn the key that's already in the ignition. I grimace and tug my arm against his. "Stop this silliness, Luke."

"Lucifer," he says, giving me a side-eye. "When you stop believing I'm the devil, then you can call me Luke, and we both know that will be never. And fuck no, I'm not releasing you. I don't trust you not to jump out when you get the opportunity."

"I'm not going to jump out of the damn car when it's the safest place to be right now, but could you drive already?"

"I don't know. Maybe I should get out and let you leave me here. That's what you want, right?"

"Damn it, Luke—"

"Lucifer."

"Drive the car," I say firmly. "This isn't a jet or a chopper, and you can't outfly the next pilot. Roads have limitations that the air does not, at least for you."

My pulse is going nuts as he grimaces and looks skyward, fingers thrumming on the dash. Any second, armed men could round that hill, and we will end up sprayed with bullets. Any second, we could die if I don't get him to drive the car.

CHAPTER TWELVE

Ana

I grab Luke's arm and twist to look up at him, my body pressing quite intimately to his. Nevertheless, that's not me playing a game. I can't move anywhere but on top of him, with the band on our wrists. "I don't want to leave you," I say. "That was never, *ever* what I wanted. I don't know what happened with my brother—"

He jerks away from my touch and cuts his gaze, staring out the window, but I don't think he's seeing anything but memories, and definitely not good ones. "I tried to explain, and you fucking shot me, Ana."

"Luke, *please*. Drive. You came for me. You saved my life. I appreciate it and—"

"You *appreciate* it?" He laughs bitterly. "Right. Good. That's sure the fuck what I want from you."

"Can we please work through all of these feelings when we're both safe? You said so yourself that we don't have time to do this now."

"Yeah, whatever." He shifts into gear and sets us in motion.

Finally, I think, sinking into the cushion, but I'm holding my breath, waiting until we turn out onto the road. He cuts right, using his left hand almost as well as he would his right if it were free, maneuvering us from one lane to the next, with no bullets in our wake. Traffic is light, and I sit up straighter again, eyeing the rearview.

"We're clear," Luke says. "No one is behind us, at least not yet. I left Savage and Adam on foot. Pull my phone out of my front pocket."

"I'm not feeling you up to get your phone," I say. "I'm not doing it."

"I'd rather you feel me up because you want to, but I'm one-handed, and I need that phone. I need to connect with my men." He flicks me a look. "Or I can pull over. It's not smart, but then I think we've proven we don't make smart decisions together, so why break from the norm?"

He went from kissing me to resentment pretty darn fast, and it punches at me rather roughly. Actually, it downright hurts, but he's also acting as if *he's* hurt, like *really* hurt, deeply, and intensely—a man who was in love and then betrayed. Guilt and confusion collide and twist me into knots. This reaction fits the man I once called a sensitive yet deadly warrior. The man I loved. Not the one monster who destroyed my world and shattered my heart.

"I got it," I say softly. "Your men aren't safe on foot. Which pocket?"

"The one next to you. And they're fine. They're resourceful. Adam told me to take the car and save you. I'd bet on them over the other guys any day."

I hope he's right because my intent tonight wasn't to get good men killed, and right now, I'm thinking Luke's men are the good guys. I reach down with my free hand, feeling for his phone. His lips curve ever so slightly. "Stop smiling."

"I'm not smiling."

I grimace, forced to use the hand that's connected to his hand. In the process, I pretty much end up holding his hand before managing to leverage myself on his leg and pull out the phone. And not without noticing the bulge in his pants. My gaze skyrockets to his, and when I want to shout my outrage, there is a part of me that is pleased that I can still turn him on. A part of me I don't want him to read.

"*Seriously?*" I challenge.

"What can I say, sweetheart? I feel like I was just taken advantage of."

"Good lord, did you really just say that?"

He ignores my remark and says, "My code is 7118. Call Adam on speakerphone."

I quickly do as he says, but the call goes straight to voicemail. "Who's next?" I ask.

"Savage."

I try the number with his named assigned with the same results, and now I'm worried. "Go back," I say quickly. "We have to go back."

He pulls into the turning lane. "Dial Blake. He's one of the founding Walker Brothers and my boss. If they called anyone, it would be him as a central coordinator."

I've heard of Walker Security. Most people in law enforcement have. They're worldwide and work almost as an extension of our operations, without quite so many rules. How appropriate, Luke, or should I say, *Lucifer*.

I tap Blake's name, and the call is answered on the first ring. "Talk to me, asshole," Blake says. "Did you save your girl? Are you both in one piece?"

"I'm not his girl," I say, "and we're safe, but we're worried about Adam and Savage."

"By *we*," Blake replies, "I assume you mean Lucifer, or did you kill him for real this time?"

"I'm here," Luke says before I can reply to that awkward confrontation. Clearly, the Walker men are protective of Luke, or it seems, *Lucifer* to just about everyone now. "Blake, meet Ana," Lucifer says. "Ana, meet Blake. Have you talked to Adam or Savage?"

"They borrowed a neighbor's car," he says, "and I've already made contact with the owners to pay for their surprise rental. Darius is safe. All the perps but one are dead. They let him go to follow him, which is what they're doing now."

I open my mouth to ask about Darius when Lucifer says, "Where's Darius?"

"He's with them," Blake answers. "Why?"

"I don't trust him," Luke replies. "As in, at all. I'm not so sure he didn't sell us out tonight, or at least Ana."

"I said he was safe," Blake responds. "I didn't say he wasn't tied up. They're dropping him at the FBI offices. Head to Breckenridge. I'll send you the address. We have a place there off the beaten path. Hole up, and the team will meet you there."

"Copy that," Luke says.

"I pinged Jake's phone. It's on his property in Estes Park. I can send a team—"

"No," Luke says. "I'll go when the time is right."

Blake's silent a beat before he says, "Any more ideas on what's going on?" Blake asks.

"Not yet, boss," Luke answers. "But I will find out one way or the other, and over as many dead bodies as necessary."

"Understood," Blake replies.

"Thank you for the help," I add quickly, sensing the conversation is about to end.

"Lucifer's the hero here, like it or not," Blake replies. "All I did was send someone along for the ride that could remove the bullet if you put another in him. Please don't. He's family, so you're family. For now. Shoot him again, the game changes. Talk soon, Luce," Blake adds and disconnects.

Silence follows.

Luke and I just sit in the darkness, our bodies touching, unspoken words, and unforgiven actions between us. There are things I want to ask and things I want to say, and I know there are things for him as well, but we have certain priorities right now, like staying alive, that force their importance upon us. His phone is still in my hand when the text message with the address comes through. "You want me to put it in Google Maps?" I ask, welcoming a way to break this silence.

"We're not going to Breckenridge," he says. "Not yet." He doesn't look at me. "Jake is lying somewhere dead. We're going to find him and honor him properly, while hoping like hell he left us a clue to find our enemy before they find us."

"Agreed," I say. "Estes Park?"

"Estes Park is the plan," he confirms.

"What about Blake? And your men?"

"Adam and Savage will come with us if I tell them the plan." He glances over at me, his blue eyes shadowed in the darkness. "And it was one thing to ask them to help me save your life, with what amounted to a ticking bomb in play. It's another to ask them to risk their lives to solve a problem that ties to my past. And yours. We do this together. We kill whoever wants us dead. And then we battle each other. Agreed?"

"Yes. Agreed."

He reaches in his left pocket, grabs a knife, and cuts me loose. It's my cue to move away from him. My eyes meet his, and once again, there are no words, but there is us. Just us. So much *us* in this car right now. Slowly, I slide to the other side of the vehicle, but it feels wrong. It was the reason why I was so scared the night I shot him. He felt so right, even then, even that night, that I knew he'd be the death of me. Like he was the death of my brother. I want to be wrong about him, but if I am, that means my brother was dirty and Luke isn't a monster. I am.

CHAPTER THIRTEEN

Ana

Luke sets the car in motion, and the space between us is remarkably far more uncomfortable than our connected hands were. The drive will be an eternal hour and a half plus drive, and travel time is without traffic and snow, which won't be an issue since it's September. It's cold, though, colder than usual for this time of year. Luke cranks the heat, the warmth somehow accentuating the tension between us.

He doesn't speak. I don't speak.

I sink back into the cushion and stare forward, my mind drifting back to the past...

It was the morning after that first meeting with Luke, a Saturday, and I'd been having coffee with Kurt and brother at Kurt's luxurious Littleton complex. It was a new Saturday thing we did since Kasey exited the Army six months before, after being ten years in. We sat at the granite island, drank coffee, talked, and then hit the firing range on the property. That morning, though, I was distracted. That kiss with Luke lingered in my mind, burning through me, consuming me. Apparently, it wasn't as impactful for him, since he didn't ask for my number.

"Whatya working on now, sugar bear?" my stepfather asks, sipping his coffee.

"Yeah, sis," Kasey chimes in. *"Whatcha working on?"*

"Nothing worth talking about," I say, still irritated that I've wasted months on surveillance, but I keep that to myself with good reason. I want Kasey to join the agency. It would be good for him. Kasey's a smart, good-looking man, charming, with blond hair and striking eyes, which makes him a woman magnet, which is a distraction he doesn't need. He seems to be struggling with what comes next in life. "Did you think about applying to the agency? You're almost at the age cutoff."

"I don't think it's for me, sis," he says. "I'm tired of the government dictating how I stand and pee, which is about how the Army ran my life. Kurt is going to hook me up with a job. Right, Kurt?"

My eyes jerk to Kurt's. "You are?"

Kurt holds up his hands. "Easy there, little one, who acts likes she's the older sibling, not the youngest. He's going to work the easy, safe jobs."

"There's no such thing," I argue, and yes, I'm protective, but I was young when Kasey decided to join the military. It feels like a miracle that I got him back now, that I'm getting to know him for the first time in our adult lives. We are the only blood family we both have. I don't think I could survive losing him.

The doorbell rings.

"Who the hell is that?" Kurt grumbles, standing and leaving his coffee behind.

Kasey holds up his hands now. "Before you lecture me, I'm going to get the coffee pot and fill our cups, but mine will have whiskey added to weather the storm of your wrath." He stands up and walks toward the kitchen.

Male voices sound in the other room, and I'm about to follow Kasey to have a serious talk with him, when suddenly my stepfather enters the room again, *followed by Luke. My heart skips a beat—God, my reactions to this man—and I am all too aware of the fact that in the light of day, he looks even better than he did last night on a dark snowy eve. His long hair is tied at his nape, his body long, lean, muscled. His eyes so damn blue and fixed on me.*

"What are you doing here?"

"I thought I might find you here," he says boldly, not giving two fucks about this being Kurt's house. He's not intimidated by him, at all. And Kurt doesn't seem to care either or he'd have already checked Luke and done so soundly.

"You got a minute?" Luke asks, motioning me toward the other room.

I'm stunned that he came here for me, but it appears that's precisely what he did. I stand, and Kurt says, "Don't leave when you're done with Ana. I want you to meet Kasey. He'd be good for that project of yours."

My concern is instant. "What project?" I ask, my eyes on Luke, who is far more likely to tell me the truth than my own family.

"I'm putting together a team to do a few private hire missions a year," he says. "It pays well, and it won't require much commitment."

I've been around Kurt's world long enough to know that "it pays well" translates to dangerous. I round the table and walk toward Luke, stopping in front of him to say, "I thought you wanted to talk in private?"

His eyes twinkle with amusement, which pisses me off. I'm not amused at all. I am, however, aware of his towering height above my five foot four inches and the woodsy, earthy scent of his cologne. "Yes," he agrees. "I do."

He backs up to allow my exit and I walk toward Kurt's office, entering through the heavy wooden door.

I step inside and around the open door, effectively turning it into a wall and a shield. Luke joins me, and before he can say a word, I lay into him, "Good money means high-risk. I do not want my brother going with you."

"You think he can't handle it?"

"I think he's very confused about who and what he wants right now, and that is not the right headspace for a high-risk mission. I want him to join the FBI."

He arches a brow. "And that's not high-risk?"

"You know there's a difference. You get paid the big payday to take risks no one else will."

"A couple of jobs and he's set-up for life."

"He'll inherit Kurt's empire. He's built the most sought-after black ops training operation in the world. He's already set-up for life."

He studies me a moment. "All right. I'll turn him down."

I blink. "Just like that?"

"Just like that."

"Kurt will—"

"He'll push, but I can handle him."

This time I don't blink. "No one else says that about Kurt except me."

He steps closer to me, the heat of his body rushing over me. "What are you doing?"

His hand cups my face, and he tilts my gaze to his. "That kiss was too good not to repeat, Ana."

My heart thunders in my chest, "Kurt has—"

Before I can warn him that there are cameras everywhere, his mouth slants over my mouth, and he's drugging me with his mouth again. I mean to push him away, I really do, but it's all I can do to not moan for the camera. And when he folds me close, his hand sliding up my back and between my shoulder blades, my breasts pressed to his chest, I melt, I really do.

Kurt's voice lifts from the distance. "Ana!"

I pull my mouth from Luke's, struggling to reclaim my own logic, especially since he's still touching me. "You can't just grab me and kiss me like that every time you see me."

"Because you don't want me to?"

"No, I—yes, I mean—" I step back, disconnect myself body from his, and do so with a shudder of regret, as I add, "Kurt." The name should say it all. It should shut him down.

"I'll handle him," he says, as if Kurt is a non-issue, when Kurt is never a non-issue.

"I don't know you, and you've done—that—twice."

"Then let's fix that. How about dinner tonight? We can get to know each other."

"No," I say. "I don't date Kurt's men. I told you that."

"And I told you. I'm not one of his men."

"You're here."

"For you."

For me.

Good Lord, could this man say anything more right when I'm trying to convince myself he's all wrong for me? "I'm not going to get to know someone who's going to go off and get killed."

"I don't die that easily, sweetheart. I promise. I'll go, but I'll be back a rich man."

"I don't care about money and I don't even want a man right now."

"And yet you kiss me like you want me. As for not wanting a rich man, sorry, sweetheart, but you'll have to settle for me and my money."

"Ana!" Kurt calls again.

"Dinner," Luke presses.

"Fine," I say. "Yes. I'll go to dinner with you."

I blink back to the present, and I suddenly can't take sitting here next to the man I thought I'd marry, with this much hate between us. I eye our location, which is just on the outskirts of the city. "I need to stop at a bathroom before we hit those desolate mountain roads."

He says nothing, but he changes lanes, and it's not long before we pull off at the next exit and pull into a truck stop. Luke parks at the side of the building, and I'm just suffocating in the man, in the memories and emotions, and even how damn good he smells. I reach for the door, but he catches my hand.

"I'm not going to let you run."

"Running isn't my style. You know that."

"Shooting me instead of facing the truth about your brother *was* running. Let me be clear, Ana. I am not your fiancé anymore. Kissing you after I just raced against a clock to save your life, even fucking you because I damn sure still want you, is not a desire to fall asleep next to you and never wake up. I don't trust you. You don't trust me. But right now, we're trying to stay alive and keep anyone else from dying."

I try to jerk my hand away. "Let go."

He does. He lets go and I'm so ridiculously conflicted over Luke that the very fact that he does both pleases me and destroys me. The only time in my life I've ever been scared has been with Luke. Scared of the next kiss, scared of him leaving and not coming back alive, scared to fall in love, scared he'll never touch me again, and that he'll be more okay with that than I will.

"Stay there. I'll come around and get you." He exits the vehicle and shuts the door.

I don't stay. I don't even think about staying. I get out of the car.

CHAPTER FOURTEEN

Lucifer

Of course, she doesn't wait. She was always hardheaded, but now that she hates me, it's tenfold. I round the hood of the car, and she's already walking toward the bathroom at the side of the store. I catch up with her and step to her side. She cast me a side-eyed glare. "I don't need an escort to the bathroom."

"You're getting one anyway."

"That whole 'shooting you was running' thing was pretty shitty."

I halt and capture her elbow, turning her around to face me. "That whole shooting me thing *was* pretty shitty, Ana."

"I called the ambulance and stopped the bleeding."

"And that makes it better?"

Her lashes lower, and her lips tremble before she looks at me again. "There's a lot neither of us can take back. Hard to believe that when we met, we were—"

"Yeah," I say. "I know." I cut my gaze and release her, hands settling on my hips. Holy hell, one way or another, she's the end of me. I look at her again. "Go to the bathroom, Ana."

"Luke—"

"*Lucifer*. I told you to call me Lucifer. Everyone does now. I'm not the man I once was, Ana. I'm the man you made me."

She pales. "Don't say that. Don't—"

59

"Speak the truth? Why? I thought that's what you wanted. The *truth*. You were screaming that, or something to that affect, before you fucking shot me. I never lied to you. Not then. Not about your brother. And not now. I was destroyed when I killed him. Even more so knowing how badly it would hurt you. But obviously, you wanted me to let him kill me. It was me you wanted to die out there that day. And I get it. He was blood. I was just someone you fucked." I turn away from her and start walking toward the bathroom.

Once I'm at the door, I stop, and I don't know why. I just feel her back there. I hesitate, and I know damn well it's because I want her to tell me I'm wrong. But she doesn't. I open the damn bathroom door and go inside, shutting it and locking it. I drag my hand through my hair and resist punching the steel door. Instead, I lean on it, pressing my hands to it, and take a deep breath. I'm trained to endure the most intense of situations, but nothing I've ever done made me ready for her. I never should have kissed her, not now, and not that first night I met her. She was right. I wasn't her kind of guy, yet, I proposed, and she said yes.

My cellphone rings, and I snag my phone from my pocket to find Blake's number. I sigh and steel myself for the inevitable. "Hey, boss."

"Why the fuck are you not in Breckenridge?"

"You only know that because you're tracking my phone like I'm a damn school kid. Stop already. This isn't a Walker job."

"What the hell, Lucifer? We face these things together. You have no idea what you're even into right now. I'm sending Savage and Adam to you."

"Don't. I'll tell you what I told Ana: it's one thing for them to help save her life with a clock ticking. It's another for me to drag them into some shit from my past that isn't even really my shit. It's her brother's."

"I thought you didn't know what this was about?"

"I have an idea."

"Talk."

"No. Fuck no. I'll go to Breckinridge after I go find Jake's body and give him a proper burial. And if you don't promise to keep Adam and Savage and anyone else away, for now, I swear to you, Blake, I'll throw this phone in the trash."

"You've got a hard head."

"I thought that was a prerequisite for working for Walker?"

"No, but it is a disease that afflicts most of you assholes, thus why my life is hell."

"Maybe because you're looking in the mirror."

"Yeah, well you need to stop talking to my wife. As for Adam and Savage, I'll hold them back, but give me something to work with. What do you think this is?"

"Not yet," I say and disconnect.

When I exit the bathroom, the women's door is open. I curse and hurry around the corner to find the car still sitting where I left it, but Ana isn't inside. Adrenaline is rushing through me, my stupidity at leaving her alone grinding through me. I enter the store, to find Ana standing at the Slurpee machine with her back to me, and my breath gushes from my lips. Thank *fuck* she's here. She didn't leave. I'm not sure what that says about where we're at together, but it does say, not as far apart as I thought, at least not on the current situation.

I start walking toward her, but some dude down the aisle to my left is yelling at his girlfriend. Men who treat women like shit grind on my nerves, but I remind myself it's not my business. Not when there are assassins on the loose, looking for me and Ana. Ana turns and faces me, with a Slurpee in her hand, her blonde hair a tousled mess, her make-up smudged under her eyes. Fuck me, she's still so damn beautiful it's killing me.

"Two hotdogs or three?" she asks, when I stop in front of her. "I know how you love your convenience store hotdogs."

The woman down the aisle yelps as if she's just been hit by the asshole who was yelling at her, and I'm at my limit. "Hold that thought," I say. "I'll be right back."

I step away from her and bring the aisle into view and the piece of shit asshole is holding the woman's hair in his hand. I'm beside him in an instant, catching his hand and twisting it in that special way, the only way you twist an asshole's hand. He yelps like a little girl and goes to his knees. "What the hell, man?! What the hell?! Let me go."

I look at the woman, who is really a girl, not more than twenty, who has blonde hair like Ana and freckles, wearing a dress with a tear in the sleeve that this guy probably created. "You okay, miss?"

"I," she breathes out, hugging herself. "I, uh, yes."

"Be smart and get away from this jerk."

The jerk is howling at this point. I glance down at his ruddy face. "Let me be clear. If you touch her again, I'll find out, and I'll kill you. You won't be the first man I kill, nor the last. Understand?"

"Yes," he pants out. "Yes. Okay. Ouuuuch. Ouch. Let me go!"

"Do you understand?" I demand.

"I said yes." I apply more pressure and he's howling again. "Yesssss. Yes!"

I free his hand. "Go now."

He hikes his hand to his chest and holds it with the other, like it's a sling, and takes off running, leaving his poor abused female friend alone. "Thank you," she says, her voice cracking with emotion. "Thank you so much."

"Do what I said. Get away from him."

"I will," she promises, but she rushes after the jerk.

I turn to find the store attendant, a heavy-set, short woman in her fifties, standing behind me. "Everything okay?"

"I purged your garbage, so I'd say that's a yes."

"Yes," she agrees. "Yes, indeed." She heads back to the register.

I round the corner to find Ana now holding a big bag she's filled with food. "I got you three hotdogs and ranch Doritos," she says as if nothing has just happened. "Killing people makes you hungry. Oh, and a Coke Slurpee. And, of course, nachos for me."

I close the space between her and me and accept the bag, staring down at her, this woman who ripped my heart out and shredded it to the point of no repair. "Amazing how well you know me now, but didn't two years ago, isn't it?"

She visibly pales. "Luke," she breathes out softly.

"Lucifer."

"I'm not calling you that."

"Don't call me Luke."

"Well, then I guess I'll just call you dude, or something stupid like that."

I grimace at her. "Let's go." I turn and walk to the register.

CHAPTER FIFTEEN

Lucifer

Ana and I exit the store and walk toward the car, and of course, the gentleman that I am, despite all that she thinks of me, I escort her to her side of the vehicle. One thing I've always loved about Ana was her ability to kick ass better than most men I know, and yet still maintain a certain feminine charm and vulnerability, especially in bed. Holy hell, the way she melted for me. I shake off the thought, juggling the bag and Slurpee to open the door for her. Or I try, but she makes it impossible. She steps in front of me.

"I got this," she says, reaching for the bag and the Slurpee, her fingers brushing mine in the process, and I swear she might as well have touched my damn cock, I get so hard. Part of me hates her, that part is obviously not in my pants.

She steps away from me, giving me room to open the door, which I do. She slides into her seat and I shut her inside, nice and safe. After which, I turn to see the jerk from inside charging at me with a gun in his hand, which he probably doesn't even know how to use. *Mother of God, will this shit never end?*

He's a short dude, but stocky and broad like a linebacker, his face one big snarl. Irritation grinds at me, and I don't wait on him to get lucky and shoot me. With a couple of long strides, I meet up with him, toe-to-toe. "You bastard," he growls, and that's all he has time to say or do. I reach out, and with a well-trained hand, take his gun, empty the bullets, and shove the weapon inside my pants.

All of this just in time to catch his fist in my hand, twist his arm, and this time, lay him flat on the ground with my foot between his shoulders. He's howling and whimpering when I say, "You're lucky I don't kill dumbasses. I'm not even going to break your arm, even though I could. Come at me again, and I'll make an exception."

He keeps howling, "Let me up. Let me up. I'll kill you."

"See, that language isn't going to help you right now." I apply a tiny bit of pressure on his joint.

"Okay, okay! I'm sorry, man. I'm sorry!"

"Where's the girl?"

"She went to the Walmart across the street. She called her dad. He's picking her up."

"You better hope that's the truth."

"It is. It is! Ouch. Ouch, man."

"Don't get up until I'm gone, or I won't make it as easy for you to get up next time. Understand?"

"Yes, man. Yes. You made me look bad to my woman. I was just trying to save face."

"Get her flowers and get out of her life, man. The end." I release him and walk back to the car, round the trunk, and climb inside.

"That was interesting," Ana says, crunching a nacho chip. "He cried, right?"

I grunt. "Pretty damn close. Let's go up the road and eat." I start the car, and a few minutes later, I pull into a bowling alley parking lot and idle the engine with the heater on.

Ana hands me a hotdog. "What you did back there, helping that girl, was a good thing."

"I didn't help her," I say. "You know as well as I do, she's going to stay with him."

"Statistically, yes, but sometimes something like what happened tonight is what makes people see the light." She holds out her nachos in my direction.

I grab a chip. "Speaking of statistics and all kinds of mumbo jumbo, how are things at the FBI?"

"I don't know," she says. "I really don't—*know.*"

I glance over at her. "You've never answered that question any differently. You realize that, right?"

"I do, actually. After you left, I went into profiler training, and I thought that would change how I feel about the agency, you know, give me more purpose."

"You're catching serial killers now?" I ask, not sure how I feel about that.

She grabs my Slurpee and takes a drink like we're still together, like she doesn't have a Diet Sprite in her drink holder. It feels familiar and right when everything about us is now wrong. Maybe it always was.

"I thought so," she says, setting the drink back down. "Which felt like I'd be doing something I could feel passionate about. Instead, I'm stuck in the white-collar crime unit unless I agree to move to another state."

"And that's a no, I take it?"

"I still have Kurt's place in Littleton. I let the local police department train out there. It keeps his legacy alive and well."

I remember the night she found out he was dead. Her knees had given out, and I'd caught her before she crashed to the ground. I held her through the tears. Shortly after, Ana took leave from work to help Kasey run the training facility, but he was drinking so much Ana couldn't take it. She thought he was safer with me than with her for once. She wanted me to take him on a few missions to help clear his head. I'd said yes, and that was the worst decision of my life.

"Why don't you leave the agency and run the training facility like you did after Kurt died?"

"Without Kurt, business faltered. He was what people came for. Renting out the property for use and recreating the training ranch is another story. I can't walk away from my badge to sit at home and do nothing."

She won't inherit from Kurt for years, so I say, "You inherited from Kasey, I assume. Why not walk away from the agency and put your all into making it something?"

"I didn't inherit from Kasey," she says. "And please don't ask for details. It's complicated. And as for the business, I'd have to hire staff, and for what, if I have no business?"

She didn't inherit from Kasey? He was rolling in the bucks just like Jake. Except, of course, he was in deep shit, that might have been deeper than I thought. If she knows that, she knows I wasn't wrong about Kasey. Or maybe she's still in denial, and eager to believe I'm a monster.

But damn it, I want to help her anyway. "If you want to go into this successfully, Walker might be interested. They're committed to constant, diverse training. I was actually in Texas training at a damn horse ranch when I got the call from Jake. And not the kind of ranch Kurt ran. Blake wants us all to know how to ride horses, in case we ever need to escape by horseback. He's ridiculously thorough about our training."

"Not a bad thing to be," she says. "But I'm pretty sure Blake doesn't like me much which is a good thing. He's supposed to be on your side."

"I don't need anyone to be on my side, Ana, and that's not how Blake rolls anyway. He's an honest, fair man."

"And Adam and Savage?"

"Adam and I met when we crossed paths, both in the same place, for different reasons. I saved his life, and then he brought me into Walker, which probably saved mine. As for Savage, he's a crazy motherfucker who tells stupid jokes, loves the hell out of his wife, and is the perfect killer you need by your side when you're trying to save lives, as twisted as that sounds."

"What does that mean?" she asks. "The part about Adam probably saving your life."

I finish off my last hotdog and ball up the paper. "I told you. I'm not the same man I was when you knew me." I glance out of the window. "It's raining, and Jake is lying who knows where. We need to go."

"Yes," she says, gathering our trash and sticking it in the backseat.

She says nothing else, and neither do I. The truth is, Jake was on a mission with Kurt when he died. They were close. He joined my team about the same time Kasey did. He was a good man, but I never shook the idea that he knew something about Kurt's death and he didn't tell us.

As if she's read my mind, Ana says, "Could all of this be connected to Kurt's death?"

Okay, she didn't read my mind. Even if Kurt has a connection, this is ultimately about Kasey being dirty. The problem is she will do anything to avoid seeing his guilt, proven by the bullet I took to the gut and her willingness to look to Kurt before Kasey. "I'm not going to give you the answer you want, Ana."

"Because you think my brother was dirty and all of this is about him."

It's not a question, so I don't answer.

Silence rules for the rest of the drive.

CHAPTER SIXTEEN

Lucifer

Darkness engulfs the vehicle, as does the rain pounding down on the windows with a force that takes me back to the night Kasey died. It was another rainy night, and we were in Egypt on a small airfield, transporting a princess under threat from one country to another. We'd intended to arrive a day early, meet with the family, and leave the next day, but bad weather and increasing danger to the princess had forced us to fly in, pick her royal highness up, and plan a rapid exit.

I believe that weather delay was ultimately why I found Kasey using me to run a second mission, working behind my back. It seemed that he was expected to do a transport to the States, and when he couldn't get to the pickup location, the item was delivered to the small airstrip where we were about to depart. I'd just ensured the princess was inside the plane and comfortable when I'd done a headcount and realized Kasey and another man on our team, Trevor, were missing.

I draw a breath and relive what had come next as I have a thousand times in the last two years....

I exit the door to the jet to find the rain is now drizzling and there's a black sedan sitting on the tarmac not far from the stairs where I now stand. Kasey is standing at the passenger door, his weapon is foolishly holstered while he leans over to speak to someone through an open window. The damn fool. The princess is a valuable commodity in these parts. He

71

knows this. I scan for Trevor, but he's out of sight, probably offering cover, which is no excuse for not communicating with me about the situation.

I use the walkie-talkie at my hip. "Jake, door. Cover me. Now."

I don't wait for his reply. Unease slices through me, an ominous blade that promises this situation is going nowhere good and fast. Hand on my weapon, I walk down the stairs, my legs eating away at the distance between myself and Kasey. I watch as Kasey accepts a small package from whoever he's talking to, and that unease I'm feeling multiplies by ten. What the fuck is this? I'm a few steps from Kasey when he eases back and turns.

"What the hell is this?" I demand, stepping toe to toe with him.

"A necklace for Ana's birthday."

He's full of shit. I step around him to the car window, which rolls up immediately. I turn back to Kasey, and the bastard punches me. I catch his arm before he can do it again. At this point, Jake's figured out the car is a problem, and he and several of my men are surrounding the vehicle with guns aimed at our visitors. The doors fly open, and a cluster of way too many men for one car exit. I'm overwhelmed just long enough for Kasey to take off for the plane where the princess awaits.

I charge after him, the rain pounding down on us again, and by the time I catch up to him, he's shot one of my men guarding the rear of the plane. My head is spinning. I can't believe Kasey just shot one of our own. I grab him and turn him toward me, and we battle. He's a good fighter, but he hasn't seen the combat I have seen. He hasn't lived to survive in the face of death the *way I have lived to survive. At one point, I have him on the ground, and I'm on top of him, punching him.*

"What the hell are you doing, Kasey?"

"I was bribed," he says. "I had to pick up a package, or everyone I know dies."

"Bullshit," I grind out. "You shot one of our men."

"Just let me up, and we'll talk, man. Come on. We're family."

He's right. He is family, but I'm no fool. He's dirty, the kind of dirty that either infects everyone around him or kills them. He reaches for his gun, and I grab it, tossing it aside. I'm about to cuff him when someone grabs me from behind, and I quickly realize it's Trevor. Kasey scrambles for his gun and aims it at me, giving me little option but to choose him or me.

"The rain stopped," Ana says beside me, snapping me back to the present. "Let's hope it stays that way. We're close, and we need a clear line of sight."

"About fifteen minutes out," I agree, but I'm still struggling to snap out of that memory that I know has something to do with the present. I just want to know what, though.

"Have you ever been to his place?" she asks.

"Jake sent me pictures after he bought it," I say. "But no, I've never seen it in person. I just know that he wanted to run those missions to buy a big place on acres of land close to his daughter."

"God, his daughter," she murmurs. "I dread telling her he's gone."

"Me too," I agree softly, guilt stabbing at me. I should never have allowed unanswered questions about Kasey's intentions that night to remain. I, of all people, know that loose ends always equal dead ends. Jake was supposed to retire a wealthy, happy man. We all were. I had a plan, a good one, too.

I exited the military with a couple of jobs already lined up and ready to pay, and a goal in mind: to do what I'd already been doing for the government but actually get myself and a team paid. A short-term in-and-out kind of deal. What I didn't have was a big enough crew. That's where Kurt came into play. He hooked me up with the right men, at the right time. The money followed. Why Kasey felt he had to run another mission, I don't know. How long he did so, I don't know, either. I've never understood it.

We all got rich. Jake got his place in Estes Park. I bought Ana a hell of a ring, and secretly bought her the dream ranch with horses she craved, which had been meant to be a wedding gift. Kasey made big money, too. The real issue burning a hole in my head is where did Kasey's money go if not to Ana?

"We're going to be expected," I say. "You know that, right?"

"Of course, we will," she replies. "It's plan B if the first trap didn't work."

I turn us down a dirt road. "We'll have to hike a few miles and approach on foot."

"Agreed," she says.

A few minutes later, I pull up between a couple of trees and park, the long branches and the dark night, sheltering our location. "Ready?" I ask.

"Of course, I'm ready. You know I'm always ready. However, I have to admit that I'm a bit surprised you brought me along for this. Why did you?"

"We both need answers and closure, and I learned the bloody hard way that my word isn't enough for you."

"Luke—"

"Sweetheart, I am Lucifer. And you better bet these motherfuckers are going to find that out before this is over. Let's go." I open the door and get out.

CHAPTER SEVENTEEN

Lucifer

They say it's hot in hell, but "they" must not have visited the high altitude of the Colorado mountains on a rainy, starless night.

Ana and I move through the forest in silence, barely a twig popping, a true testament to the wet ground and our training. When finally, we round a mountain top and find coverage inside a line of trees, it's only to find Jake's place dark, not a light on in sight.

"Unnaturally dark," Ana whispers. "He would have had on at least one light when they attacked him, and he wasn't alive to turn anything off."

"Agreed," I say, and this only serves to confirm what I warned her about in the car. This is a trap.

"Should we wait until dawn?" she asks. "We're almost there."

"I don't think there's a good answer to either waiting or going now."

"Let me call in law enforcement. They'll light up the place and find the body. With my badge and a claim that you're a consultant, it will allow us full access."

"And what happens when they start shooting at the small-town police?"

"That would start a manhunt. Do you honestly think whoever this is has proven to be that stupid?"

"The police will make this complicated."

"My badge says otherwise. Let's make the call."

"And if someone is working against you inside the FBI, even beyond Darius?"

"I won't call it in to my boss, not now. Not until we're gone, and I have a protected line."

I hand her my cell. "Use mine for the local call, and later to call your boss. My team scrambles our lines. They're not traceable."

She accepts my phone and, after a quick search, makes her call. It doesn't take her long to have the police chief on the phone. Funny how the phrase "FBI" gets everyone's attention. It reminds me that Ana was always a rule follower. Me, not so much, which is probably a part of why she so easily believed I was dirty and her brother was not. But there's a difference between crossing lines and completely whiting them out.

"We believe this is a trap," Ana is saying next to me. "Light the place up, and I know you're a small force, but I need as many men as you can spare. Me and my man will go in first to protect your own." She listens a minute. "Really? You have dogs? Yes. Bring them. Right. We'll stay undercover until you arrive. We'll need a few minutes to get to you." She disconnects. "I can't believe they have dogs in this small town. Apparently, they have an ex-cop who trained police dogs living in the city, and he basically rents his dogs to them. They're going to light up the place and send in the dogs first." She hands me my phone back.

"Let's hope the bastards don't shoot the dogs."

"Please don't say that. Don't even put it out in the universe. I'll lose my shit. You know I will. And on a separate note, I'm worried about this getting back to his daughter before we can tell her. Then there's also the other side of the coin, where I worry they went after her, too, and we need to get an officer out there."

"If they went after her, she's dead. If they didn't, we need to tell her ourselves after dealing with the crime scene. How soon will they be here?"

"Ten minutes for the police. Fifteen for the dogs. They're going to hold back and wait on the dogs." There's a shift in the air that might as well be a twig popping. My eyes cut through the darkness to meet Ana's, and I motion for her to move, and to do it now.

CHAPTER EIGHTEEN

Lucifer

Just as Ana starts to move, the glint of yellow eyes captures my attention.

"Stop," I order urgently before the coyotes think we're running and see us as fearful prey just asking to be chased.

Ana freezes, and I add, "Coyotes," rather than a coyote, because where there is one, there are always more.

"Wonderful," Ana replies, the calmness in her tone coming from years of survival training Kurt all but beat into her, the bastard. "The teeth of a dog or the bullet of an asshole," she adds. "Not much of a choice."

She's not wrong, I think.

In a perfect situation, we handle the coyotes and move on, but to do that, we have to get big and loud to scare the animals off, which pretty much places a bullseye on our backs. But we can't do nothing. Big it is. "Turn to face them and stand up on three." I don't wait for a reply. "One. Two. Three."

We both move at the same time, our backs to the house as we raise our hands, moving them around, almost as if we're saying, "Here we are. Shoot us." As for the coyotes, at least three of them snarl, a sure indicator that our plan has failed. Ana and I pull our weapons at the same time. "You got a rock you can throw?" I ask, scanning my feet to find anything helpful and coming up dry.

"Nothing," she says. "No rocks. Not even a stick."

I curse under my breath because I'm going to have to charge at the coyotes, and that might mean I end up shooting at least one of the pack, and that's a really shitty endgame. This is their land, over our land, and I try my damnedest to respect that fact, but the longer we stand here, the more likely we end up with bullets in our bodies. "You know what I'm going to do," I say softly.

"You sure about that?" she asks, obviously reading my plan and not keenly.

"Any other suggestion?"

Sirens shrill to the rear of our position, and lights set the sky to an extreme glow. The cavalry has arrived. The coyotes react and scamper away. Ana and I both kneel for cover. "Call the number I called and tell them we're coming down," Ana whispers.

A few minutes later, we're safely standing at the gates of the property and doing so with no bullet holes in our bodies. We're also in the company of the Estes Park small town cavalry. And for a small town, they've gone all out. There are four patrol cars and a few random vehicles present, two of which are hitched to a trailer that holds the spotlights scanning the property.

A tall, lanky man with a beard greets us, and Ana pulls out her badge, offering him a glance. "Agent Banks," he greets after checking her credentials. "I'm Chief Montgomery. Glad you made it to us safely."

"Thanks for your quick response," she replies. "We actually had coyotes at our back right about the time you turned up those lights. Well-timed, I must say."

"Coyotes are bold little fuckers around these parts," he says, "but they don't like people, unless they decide to eat you." He doesn't laugh but he does move quickly to what's on all of our minds right now. "I hope like hell you're wrong about Jake being dead."

"She's not," I say, interjecting myself into the conversation. "Whoever did this shot him while he was on the phone with me, trying to warn me that they were coming for me and Agent Banks next."

Ana makes a quick introduction, covering my ass and her own with, "This is Luke Remington, consulting on the case for Walker Security, but this is personal to us both, Chief. Luke has connections to my stepfather at The Ranch training facility in Denver."

"Your stepfather is Kurt Banks?" he asks, making it clear that he knew Jake well enough to know exactly who and what we're talking about.

"Was," Ana replies tightly. "He's been gone for years now." She doesn't give him time to comment, adding, "We're going to need to be the first to walk the scene for a multitude of reasons, including the safety of your men."

"We're a small force here," he says. "Unlike some of the big city folks, we don't mind assisting the FBI and backing you up."

"Chief!" someone calls out. "The dogs have something at the house!"

"I didn't know the dogs had gone in," Ana responds and she doesn't sound pleased. "I need you to tell everyone who isn't controlling a dog to stand down, Chief."

"Yes, ma'am," the Chief replies. "We'll get you in and out of there safely."

I'm not a take orders kind of guy, but she's sexy as hell bossing everyone else around. It reminds me of why I fell in love with her. She held her own with me from the first moment I met her in that corner store. I didn't just want to fuck her. I wanted to own her. Instead, she owned me. And it was almost the death of me, quite literally.

"Shine the lights left and right," I say, and it's not a suggestion. "We need to blind anyone who might want to pick us off."

"Holy hell," the Chief says. "You really think that's going to happen?"

"No," I say, "because you're going to point those lights in their lines of sight."

The chief nods and hurries away, shouting out random commands. The lights are turned on and a young man, maybe twenty, in jeans and a puffer jacket, offers us police raincoats with hoods. "I'm Allen. My dad, the chief, said the hoods will hide your identity. I'd offer you bullet proof vests, but I'm afraid we don't have extra. Those lights should blind anyone who wants to fire, regardless of a jacket or a vest."

"Thanks," Ana says, accepting hers. "Can we get gloves for the crime scene?"

"Yes, ma'am. I'll get those for you." Allen hurries away.

Ana and I shrug into our new garments. "Thank God for this," Ana says as we lift our hoods. "Because I didn't feel the cold when our adrenaline was pumping but now that we stopped, I do."

"I think we're about to get a whole lot colder and not from the weather," I say. "Because we both know what those dogs found."

"Jake's dead," she supplies, "and if his killers have their way, we'll be next, if they get lucky."

"As Kurt would say, skills are mastered. Luck is not. We'll live. The asshole who killed Jake will not. I'm going to kill him, and just to be clear, I don't give two fucks about your badge or what you think of me after."

CHAPTER NINETEEN

Lucifer

Ana stares at me, the air snapping between us. I don't know what she sees when she looks at me anymore. Man? Monster? Lucifer? I don't care anymore, either. I am who I am, and that isn't anyone either of us recognizes as me, and she doesn't even know how deep that change runs.

"I don't know how you expect me to react to that," she says.

"I don't care how you react, Ana. Agent Banks. I am who I am. I'm not apologizing. I'm not asking you for permission. I'm telling you what I'm going to do. That means I find the bastard I talked to on the phone, kill him and his men, and do so painfully. If you want to try to arrest me for it, fuck it. Let's do this."

Allen appears and offers us gloves. "You're clear to go in."

We accept the gloves and he hurries away.

I shove the gloves in my pocket. "As I said, let's do this." I start walking. Ana falls in beside me.

"I loved Jake," she says. "He was like a father to me. I'm just as invested in doing right by him as you are."

I don't pretend to know what that answer means, and I don't reply. She's lost everyone that resembled family in her life, including me, at least in her mind. But the reason she lost me is exactly why I can't offer her comfort. It wouldn't matter. Not coming from the devil himself.

I focus on the sidewalk we're traveling on toward a dark blue house with a steepled roof, horse stables to our left, and the hilltop where we hid earlier, to our right. This place was Jake's dream home that will now become his daughter's. *If* she can stomach living in the place he died.

We reach the front door, and a tall Black man and a German Shepard greet us. "I'm Jack's human," he informs us, offering us no other name. "He's got a hit inside the house. You want him to go in first, or do you want to handle it?"

"We've got it," I say. "Keep your pup out here and safe."

The dog's "human" as he likes to call himself gives us a nod. "Much appreciated."

I draw my sidearm and step forward, not about to give Ana the option of going in first. I reach for the knob and the dog whines.

"What is he telling us?" Ana asks quickly.

"He's a cadaver dog," is all the man says.

In other words, he's not trained to warn us about the living. He's trained to find what's left of those who are not. It's a shitty confirmation of Jake's death, which is also a shitty reality. I enter the house into a grand living room with vaulted ceilings and so far, no sign of Jake. Ana steps to my side and then starts walking toward the kitchen. I grimace. Stubborn woman doesn't know how to follow the leader and stay behind me. Ever.

I'm beside her when we both enter the kitchen to find Jake sprawled on the floor, face down, a trail of blood where he's tried to drag himself across the tile. His phone is also on the floor, by the door, just beyond his now stiff fingers.

"The bastards left him alive and taunted him with the phone," I say, closing the space between me and Jake. I kneel beside his body and scan for anything that tells me who to go kill right now.

Ana does the same, though I assume her motives are a little more pure, both of us keeping our hands on our knees to avoid contaminating the evidence. Voices lift in the outer room, and Ana stands. "I need to go give them direction."

I push to my feet as well. "I'm going to look around." She opens her mouth as I pull out my gloves. "I know, Agent Banks."

"Stop calling me that."

"Lucifer and Agent Banks. We've come a long way, baby, now haven't we?"

Her lips press together and she turns away from me, walking briskly toward a law enforcement officer waiting on her in the doorway. My gaze returns to Jake's body, my mind traveling to the past. To the hellish moment after I'd scrambled with Kasey for a gun. I'd snagged the weapon, but I'd been jumped again. When I'd freed myself, Kasey not only had another gun, he had the princess. He'd held his weapon at her head and I saw the trapped rat in a cage. I knew the moment it became me and her or him.

I killed him.

The princess continued to scream, terrified and covered in blood.

I'd motioned to one of my other men, Christian. "Get her inside to safety."

He'd done as I ordered. Jake had stepped to my side then. "You had no choice, son."

I couldn't go there right then. I couldn't think about Ana right now or we might all end up dead. "Where is the package?" I'd asked.

"It seems it and Trevor are missing. And I don't think we have enough men left to hunt for him. We need to get in the air. We need to leave that little bitch here to die."

He'd been right.

And that's exactly what we did. We'd left that little bitch to die, and yet somehow, he'd made it back to Colorado before we did. He'd gone to Ana and played her. He'd told her I killed Kasey and flipped the entire story. I was the one running dirty jobs, according to him. She'd known him for years longer than me, and somehow, that was enough for her to believe him.

And if Trevor hadn't died in that car accident a year and a half ago, I'd be hunting him right now.

As for Jake, he didn't stay around to talk sense into Ana when she wouldn't listen to reason. He wanted out. He got out. Or so he thought.

My gaze lifts to the archway where Ana has now disappeared through, and that's probably a good thing right about now, considering the anger burning through me at her and myself. Maybe, just maybe, if we had both handled what happened differently, Jake wouldn't be dead.

CHAPTER TWENTY

Lucifer

There's nothing to find in Jake's house that helps us catch a killer or decipher a hitlist. I look. Ana looks. The police look. To complicate matters, CSI is delayed and arriving from a bigger city. Towns of six thousand just don't have those kinds of resources. With limited options for proceeding, at least here at Jake's place, Ana and I are back outside the house, standing with the chief, when a car screeches to a halt. A moment later, a woman exits, wearing pajama pants and a sweater, and screaming, "Daddy! Daddy!"

Olivia, Jake's daughter, who I've met on several occasions in the past.

"Sometimes I hate small town word of mouth. I really want to throw up right now," Ana says, "but I'll talk to her."

She takes a step in Olivia's direction, and I catch her arm. "No," I say firmly. "I need to talk to her." I don't give her a chance to debate. I step around her and close the space between me and Olivia, who is presently standing in front of a police officer, shouting at him. She appears to be alone, with no coat on, and her long dark hair damp from the light rain that's now falling again.

She must sense my approach as she turns, her eyes going wide, her face crumpling in a new round of tears. Me being here sends a message. She knows what that means. "No," she howls as I get closer. "No! No! No!

Don't you even say it." She points at me. "Don't you even say it!"

Holy hell, carve me into pieces already. I step in front of her and she punches at me, fighting anything and anyone who can speak her new reality. I catch her arms. "I will do anything I can to help you."

She throws her arms around me and sobs. I hold onto her, and I swear, time is eternal as she cries until I think she will cry herself into her own grave. An EMS team approaches, and I ease her back a bit. "Let the medical staff give you something to calm down a bit, and then we can talk."

"We don't need to talk," she argues. "I just need the facts. Did someone kill him? Was this murder?" Her voice is raspy, raw, angry. Her eyes are bloodshot and swollen.

I slide out of my jacket and wrap it around her. "Yes."

"And what are you going to do about it?" she demands.

I wave away the medical staff. "What do you want me to do, Olivia?"

"I want you to kill anyone involved in this. He was happy. We were so happy to be together again. Family is supposed to be together. And I'm *pregnant.* He was going to be a grandpa. He was so excited and now he will never know his grandson."

And her mother's been gone for years.

Her voice lifts. "Do you hear me? He won't know his grandson. How am I supposed to do this alone?" She sobs, but her spine straightens, her lips curling around her teeth. "Kill the bastard who did this."

"I will. You have my word," I promise easily. I will kill anyone involved in this. "Now, let's get you to the medics, okay?"

"Yes," she whispers. "Yes, please give me something to numb what I feel right now."

I lift my hand and motion toward the EMS truck, but then hold up one finger to indicate I only want just *one* medic to come to her now. I don't want her overwhelmed. "Where's your husband?"

"Dead," she says. "A tractor rolled over him last month."

Holy hell, I can't take it. This woman's pain is just too much, but I don't tell her I'm sorry. It won't do anything but imply pity, and she's not a woman who wants to be pitied. That's not how Jake raised her, and that's definitely not how Jake lived.

The medic joins us, a tall, red-headed man. Once he's checked her vitals, it's not long before he injects her with something to calm her down. During the process, my cellphone keeps ringing, which I ignore, and someone offers me another jacket that I slide on.

When I finally leave, confident Olivia in good hands, I leave her with the intent of getting the hell out of here. Ana is quick to step to my side. "Is she okay?"

"No, she's not fucking okay. I'll see you in the car. Have someone bring you to me when you're ready."

She catches my arm and damn it to hell, I feel it all the way to my damn cock, which apparently is immune to the death and hate all around me right now. "You can't walk alone when you're on a hitlist."

"Why do you care, Ana? They'll just finish what you started." I jerk away from her and begin walking again.

She rushes forward and steps in front of me, her blue eyes tormented. "Don't say that. I do *not* want you to die."

"And yet, you tried to kill me." I step around her and start walking again.

She's back by my side in a few beats, keeping pace with my long strides. "You walk. I walk."

Whatever, I think. She does what she wants to do. Nothing I say will change that. I know that now. I should have seen it in the past.

However, it's not only Ana who won't let me go, it seems. The chief appears by my side. "What's happening right now?"

"I'm leaving," I say.

"We have to leave before we get your team killed," Ana says, leaning forward to speak to him from across my body. "I'll call you once we're undercover."

"Don't walk," he says. "We'll drive you to your car."

My jaw clenches. "I don't need a ride."

"We're fine," Ana says. "I'll call you soon."

"All right," the chief murmurs. "Seems foolish, but all right." He stops walking.

Ana keeps pace with me. There was a time when her being by my side was everything. Hell, I hate that it still feels good to have her beside me. I don't even know how that's possible. The woman shot me, but then, I did kill her brother. Even if it was justified, the hardcore reality here is that there is no way she can live with that. I can barely live with it myself.

At this point, we've left the busy crime scene and we're walking down the dark highway, but I don't seek shelter. I dare whoever came at Jake to come at me or Ana. I swear to God, I'll drag them to hell with me and enjoy every second.

CHAPTER TWENTY-ONE

Lucifer

The haze of the new day lingers over the mountaintop, while the sun illuminates our path and allows our enemies to see us coming. Suits me just fine, too. I prefer to see the faces of the men who killed Jake when I kill them, so bring it. Bring it now. Why drag this out? But a mile up the road, it's clear I'm not going to get that lucky. Ana and I climb into the car without anyone daring to fuck with us. Chicken shit bastards. They probably ran when the cavalry arrived, and that's fine. I'll hunt them down if that's how they want to play this game.

With that hunt in mind, I don't waste any time pulling us onto the main road while Ana twists around to check our rear. "So far, so good," she says, about a mile into the ride, but we both know that doesn't mean someone isn't waiting somewhere in our forward path for us to approach. That's how chicken shits operate. They shoot you in the back if they get the chance.

My cellphone rings again and this time I answer the call without even looking at the caller ID. "Where are you?"

At the sound of Blake's voice, I say, "In the car, getting the hell out of Estes Park. You're on speaker with Ana."

"You found Jake?" he asks.

"Yeah. We found him face down on his kitchen floor in a puddle of his own blood. We also found his pregnant daughter who just lost her husband a month ago."

"Oh fuck," Blake murmurs at the same time Ana says, "Oh, my God. I didn't know that."

"That's a one-way path out of Estes Park," Blake comments, keeping us focused. "You sure you're not being followed?"

"For now, yes," I confirm. "What waits up the road for us is yet to be seen."

"Assume you're being tracked, which means you can't go straight to Breckenridge. I'm texting you a location in Boulder to dump your car. I have a private driver picking you up. Have him take you to some random location, walk a bit, and then Uber to the hotel I've already booked. There will be a new car waiting for you, and the keys will be under the driver's seat. I'm texting you all the details now."

"Wow," Ana says. "You think of everything, don't you?"

"It's life or death," Blake replies. "And, Ana, there are plenty of clothes and supplies in Breckinridge. Take what you need until you can buy some new things to get you by. Lucifer has a company card. Use it. You can't use your own."

"You don't have to do that," Ana says quickly.

"You can't use your cards. You need to consider yourself in a safe house situation until we know otherwise."

"Right," Ana replies, her voice tight. "Yes. I know. Thank you. That's generous and appreciated. I'm not quite sure who in my inner circle to trust right now."

"I told you," Blake replies. "You matter to Lucifer, and you're family until you prove otherwise."

Ana looks skyward and then cuts her gaze, obviously affected by Blake's words.

Maybe she hates the idea of being part of a family that is mine. Maybe she regrets the fact that she made sure we couldn't ever be what we once were ever again. Maybe the very idea of being called my family disgusts her. Hell, I don't know what is going through Ana's mind. I just know that she does matter to me. Too damn much considering our history.

"Do you have anything on the hitlist?" I ask, moving on, to what should matter right now.

"Not yet," he says. "I do have addresses and updates on every man who worked for you, but I haven't made contact yet. We have to consider any one of them could be involved in this."

"On the other hand, any one of them could be on the hitlist, too. I need to warn them."

"You want me to handle it?"

"No. Send me numbers. I'll call them, and I'll feel them out when I do."

"You sure? You have about twenty men on the list. I'm pretty damn good at feeling people out. I can record the exchanges. You really need to focus on keeping you and Ana alive right now."

"Right. Yeah. Do it."

"Good decision," he approves. "Call Adam. He wants to talk to you and Ana."

"Anything on Darius?" Ana asks anxiously. "Is he dirty? Did he set us up?"

"We don't know yet," Blake replies. "Any communication I can access looks clean, but he could have been using a throwaway phone, so that doesn't mean a lot. I'm diving deeper. And so are Adam and Savage. But the very fact that you have to ask me that tells me there's something more to this story."

"A gut feeling," Ana says, "which I've learned never to discount. He's been acting a little off, and I can't even explain what that means."

"I know what it means," Blake assures her. "And you're right. Never ignore a gut feeling."

"I'll call Adam now," I say.

"Don't get killed," Blake orders. "I'm sending you everything promised now."

"Great, and if I die, Blake, cremate me and have Savage tell a stupid joke before you dump my ass wherever the hell you want." On that note, I disconnect, glance in my rearview, and then dial Adam. I get his voicemail before I try to reach Savage. Same story.

At this point, we're twenty-five minutes to Boulder. I need food and a few hours of rest before taking on those narrow-ass roads on the way to Breckinridge. I can fly through hell and back, but don't make me drive it without food and sleep.

"I hadn't talked to Jake in months," Ana says. "You know he and his daughter had a strained relationship for years. They'd just really found each other again. And now he's gone. We should do something for her."

"We are," I say. "We're going to kill the bastards that killed him. After that, we'll go back and tell her. I promise you, she'll rest a little more peacefully."

"But now she's alone in a small town."

"Judging by how fast she found out about her father, she's not alone."

"Killing them might give her peace but it won't offer her comfort. Maybe we could take her something that reminds her of Jake. I don't know what, but something. I guess there's really nothing." She hesitates, "You still think this has something to do with my brother?"

I glance over at her. "I know it does."

"How can this be about Kasey?" she argues. "He's been dead two years."

And her father has been dead three, and for the first time right now, I'm connecting those dots between Kasey and Kurt, and there's something dirty. I respected Kurt. I liked Kurt. But Kurt had a dark side, and so did Kasey. He inherited The Ranch and the business, yet had no money to pay the taxes, which never made sense to me. Kurt wasn't a man who forgot to tie up ends, but nevertheless he did. Maybe he thought Kasey would bring in that income with the business. Kasey had skills, he was well-known as Kurt's stepson, but even with Jake by his side, they lost business. Prideful bastard didn't tell me or Ana, until it was too late.

I'm back to Ana won't inherit anything from Kurt until she's thirty-six, four years from now, and she doesn't even know *what* she'll inherit. The documents are sealed, but it should be millions. Kurt made a fortune in just the time I knew him. At the time of his death, holding back Ana's inheritance seemed like a Kurt thing to do. He wanted Ana to learn to survive on her own efforts. He wanted her to have her dream, her life, not be consumed by his. He trained her because after losing her mother, he didn't want her to end up dead. Not sure how her joining the FBI rather than running The Ranch made that happen, but he couldn't control her life. That's the point. He didn't want his world to own her world. His world was always going to own Kasey's.

It all made sense at the time, but now I'm not sure there isn't more to it.

Was there another reason he wanted to keep Ana away from The Ranch?

"Luke," Ana presses, snapping me out of my reverie.

Luke again, I think, but I let it go. I've given up on her calling me Lucifer. Hell, she can call me whatever she wants. It won't change what she thinks of me. "All of this is related to Kasey, Ana. The end. I'd risk my life on it, and as you remember, I already have. But the bottom line is, both of us might as well have pulled the trigger and killed Jake. Our dysfunctional relationship made you shoot me, and then I walked away rather than making sure the trouble died with your brother."

"You mean *I* did this."

"No. You didn't make me walk away. I'm responsible for my own decisions. *You* didn't do this. *I* didn't do this. *We did.*"

CHAPTER TWENTY-TWO

Ana

We did this.

We killed Jake, or rather, we got him killed.

Together, Luke and I were the perfect storm of events that led us to a place of death and destruction. But ultimately, I started the storm, and the idea that I'm the reason Jake is dead, and his pregnant daughter no longer has a father and her unborn child a grandfather is almost too much for me to stomach.

Next to me, Luke tries to reach Adam and Savage again to no avail, trying to catch them when they can talk and we can as well, and cranking up the radio with country tunes in between attempts. He's filling the empty space with anything but our words and I can't say I blame him.

I almost killed him.

That entire week haunts me. I lost my brother. I blamed Luke when I'd never thought him capable of such a thing. Being with him again only drives that tormenting point home.

My mind goes back to that horrible, brutal night. Trevor had gotten to me first. I'd been at work when he'd called. *"I need to see you now. Where are you?"*

"I'm on duty. I won't be home until late tonight."

"I need to see you now. It's urgent."

There is evident panic in his voice, and Trevor isn't a panicking kind of guy. "What's wrong?"

"Just meet me at your house. Now, Ana. It needs to be now."

I squeeze my eyes shut and block out the memory, I don't want to remember, but I cannot escape it. But there is no denying that the right here and now circles back to that week. Unbidden, a mental image of Jake lying face down on his kitchen floor in a pool of his own blood tortures me. He was my *godfather*, the last of those I considered my family.

Inwardly, I shake myself and open my eyes only to realize we're already inside Boulder's city limits. My gaze goes to the rearview mirror.

"We're clear," Luke says, reading my intent. "And this is our drop-off spot." He turns us into an office complex on a hilly incline, with heavy tree cover and a cluster of at least a dozen vehicles. Once we're parked in the rear corner, with no other cars near us, he kills the engine.

"Do we even know who we're meeting?" I ask, antsy that our present location could prove the perfect camouflage for us to hide or for someone else to kill us.

"We're not meeting anyone. This guy is a driver and nothing more. He doesn't know us, he won't ever know us, and I like it that way."

As if on cue, a black sedan pulls to the front of the building. It's always a black sedan, and I always fear that with the desire to be nondescript and basic, we're actually being quite noticeable.

"That's our ride, sweetheart," Luke says. "Stay here. Let me make sure I feel good about the driver." He leaves the keys in the ignition and exits the vehicle.

Concerned he might need back-up, I open my door and exit as well. The morning is mild, the moment casual, if not for my awareness of my weapon in my holster and my two-day-old clothes. I'm dirty. I'm exhausted. I'm twisted in emotional knots. But as Kurt would have said, none of these are an excuse for letting down my guard.

I scan the area and then watch Luke approach the idling vehicle, his confident saunter and broad shoulders stirring a reaction in me that, putting history aside, should not even be possible for obvious reasons. But, then again, my reaction to all things Luke Remington has always been unexplainably, overwhelmingly present, and impossible to fight.

And that, it seems, has not changed.

I still feel a flutter in my belly every time he looks at me.

I still notice every time the dimple on his left cheek quirks in that sexy way it does when he's amused or irritated.

I still feel his every little touch with such intensity that I might as well be naked and in his arms.

And when he kissed me—my God, when *he kissed me*—I melted. How could I not? He still kisses me like I'm the only thing he breathes for. Even after what I did to him.

In a demonstration of Luke's approval of the driver, he opens the rear door of the vehicle and motions for me to join him. I begin walking toward him. He doesn't turn away. He stands there, watching my approach, and just like the first night I met him when he'd leaned on his bike and watched my every step, he watches me in an uninhibited, sexual way and doesn't make any attempt to mask it. Luke never hid who he was or what he wanted from me. And there was a time not so long ago when being what he wanted was everything. The truth is that in moments like this when I'm in the heat of his presence, it's impossible not to be consumed by him. I didn't even know it was possible to react to one person in the intense way I react to Luke.

When the space between us is gone, I stop in front of him and our eyes lock for the smallest of seconds. The impact is this crazy wicked mix of love, hate, lust, and passion that is downright combustible.

I watch his jaw tighten, almost as if he's pushing back against the impact of me and him, the impact that is us together.

"Get in," he orders, his tone clipped, his irritation at what just passed between us crystal clear, as if he wants to hate me, and in turn, hates that he can't. Not completely.

I climb inside the rather small backseat of the car-for-hire and he shuts me inside. The driver doesn't greet me, and that's just fine by me. I don't want him to know my name, face, or voice. I want to be in and out of this car. A few moments later, Luke joins me in the backseat, and we are ridiculously close, to the point that once he's shut the door, I can feel his body heat.

My hand is on the seat and his goes to the same place, and there is a collision of skin against skin. And as is always, with any touch by this man, I feel that tiny little spark in every part of me.

Without even thinking, I look at him and he looks at me, and then a million tiny pieces of our history play between us, but they are broken because we are broken. Shattered into tiny pieces, to the point that I'm not sure we can ever mend—neither apart nor together.

I did this, I think, and I look away, pulling my hand back and setting it on my leg. Both of my hands are on my legs now, and I am staring at the bare finger that not so long ago was adorned with a stunning ring that symbolized our never-ending bond.

The one that ended—only it doesn't feel as if it ended at all.

I guess it's true that the line between love and hate is thin.

Only, I don't want hate to be what is between us. I never wanted this for us. I just wanted us.

CHAPTER TWENTY-THREE

Ana

Luke has the driver drop us at a random hotel, which is not the hotel where we plan to stay the night. We walk inside, watch the driver pull onto the highway, and then exit again, with Luke glancing at the Google maps app on his phone. "There should be a Taco Bell a mile up the road. We can eat there and call an Uber."

"Food sounds really good right about now," I say as we start walking. "And so does sleep, but I know that's not in the near future."

"A good hour, at least," he confirms. "We're going to have to Uber around like fools before we settle in for a rest."

"Run around in circles and confuse the hell out of whoever thinks they know where you are and where you'll go next," I say, quoting Kurt.

"Kurt and his training saved my life more than once."

And yet, Kurt supposedly made a mistake that got him killed on his final mission. That's always sat wrong with me, but then again, he was my father figure, no matter how much I sometimes hated his coldness and the way he pushed me. Accepting that he wasn't invincible was highly devastating. Accepting your brother is dirty, on the heels of that loss, nearly impossible. Kasey wasn't a bad person. He had bad shit happen in the military, stuff he never explained, but he couldn't sleep most nights, he had a short temper, and he just didn't accept defeat easily. He also saw defeat where others saw obstacles. So much so that he was willing to do whatever he had to, to avoid his perceived failure. To him, whatever it took, meant *whatever* it took. I tried to help him. I loved him. He was my brother. Luke knew how much he meant to me so finding out the man you loved is the one who took his life is confusing and terrifying.

Enough to make me stupid.

There are things I need to tell Luke, but right now, when we must stay alert and watch for trouble, is not that time. I'll talk to him at the hotel. For now, we walk, but a mile isn't that far, and soon enough, we're at a table eating our food.

It's actually quite surreal, sitting across from him and sharing a meal as if we're still us and not whatever this is that we are now.

"You have dirt all over your cheek," Luke says, surprising me by reaching across the table and rubbing it off my cheek.

My breath hitches with the connection, and when he says, "All gone," and starts to pull away, I don't let him.

I catch his hand. "Luke—"

"You just can't get my name right, can you?" he challenges, but he doesn't pull away from my touch.

My heart is racing, and I want to say so many things to him. I *need* to say so many things. "I just—I need—"

"Be careful what you ask for, Ana," he warns softly. "You might regret it."

"I have enough regrets to last a lifetime," I whisper.

"And yet you never called me."

He's wrong. I did. I called him. Not from my phone. And once, he picked up. I heard his voice, and the ground spun under my feet. The next time I tried, his number was disconnected.

"I did, actually."

He studies me, his lashes lowering, half-veiled, his expression unreadable. "When?" he asks softly.

"Does it matter when?"

"It matters," he assures me.

His cellphone rings, and I want to scream in frustration because I know he has to get it. "Saved by the bell," he says softly, and I'm not sure if he's talking about him or me, or perhaps both of us.

He untangles from my hand, and as he answers the call, I can almost feel the wall between us thickening.

"Yeah, Adam," he says into the phone. "Yeah. We'll call you when we get to a safe place." He glances at his watch. "About forty-five minutes. Right. Yeah. Later." He disconnects. "Adam wants us to call him when we get to our room."

My spine straightens. "Us?"

"That's what he said, and no, I don't know why, but if it were urgent, he'd have told me." He starts cleaning up. "We need to get moving."

He's right. We do. But I can't help regretting the moment that we just lost.

I hate him, I do. He killed my brother, but there is also no denying that my heart bleeds without this man in my life. I still love him. And not even blood or water will wash that away. I know. I tried. And I failed. Now, I'm not sure I'm even trying anymore.

The next forty-five minutes includes two Ubers, a stop at a store on foot to grab a few items, including suitcases to look the role of travelers, and finally, we arrive at our destination hotel. The St. Julien is a five-star hotel that is both stunning on the outside and on the inside, with its mountain views and luxurious lobby.

"The nicer the hotel, the higher end the security," I say, rolling my small suitcase behind me.

"Just like Kurt taught us," Luke supplies a moment before we step up to the check-in counter, where he offers the clerk a fake identity. "Reservation under the name Wright."

"One moment," the clerk says, typing a moment before she says, "Welcome Mr. and Mrs. Wright," making the façade of husband and wife that Luke must already be aware of now awkwardly crystal clear to me as well.

"You'll be on the eleventh floor," the woman continues, "and I'm sorry I cannot accommodate your reservation request for an upgrade to a suite. There's a convention in town, and you got our last room."

Room, I repeat in my head, as in singular. It seems Luke and I will be sharing a room, which makes sense, of course. He doesn't trust me not to run, and we're pretending to be what we once might have been: a happy, married couple who would sleep in the same bed.

CHAPTER TWENTY-FOUR

Ana

Luke and I step into the empty hotel elevator and stand side-by-side. Once the doors seal, it's as if a countdown starts. Three. Two. One.

We turn and face each other, the tiny space punched with ten thousand intimate, sexy moments. The air is thick. The baggage heavier than anything we have in our nearly empty suitcases. For long seconds, a full minute perhaps, we don't speak. We just stare at each other, but the floors tick by as heavily as the unspoken words and unrealized emotions hanging between us.

"There was only one room," he says. "Pretty much in the whole city. Blake warned me earlier."

"And you didn't warn me." It's not a question.

"I didn't want you to run."

"The running thing again? Really? I've never run from anything. That's not who I am."

"I think I've made it clear that I disagree on that point, but in case you've forgotten my point of view: you ran from the truth. If I'd died that day two years ago, Ana, and if I didn't stand right here right now, you might have gone to your own grave believing lies."

"I didn't mean to shoot you."

His eyes sharpen with his tongue. "Liar."

"Now I'm a liar?"

"You're too skilled to accidentally pull the trigger, sweetheart, so dump that bullshit and be honest with yourself and me."

"If you believe that, why not go to the police? Why did you lie about what happened?"

"The why doesn't matter. The reason? I saved your badge," he says. "Just be thankful I did."

The elevator dings. "Let's go call Adam."

I'm obviously not the only one eaten up with hate. He is, too, and I don't think he would feel what he feels if he'd coldheartedly killed Kasey. "Luke—"

"*Lucifer*, Ana. Lucifer. I get that you always refused to call me that and refused to see me as that person, but you always knew who I was. And I'm more him than ever. You of all people know that. You made that clear." He doesn't give me time to reply. "Let's go call Adam," he repeats, catching the elevator door as if the action is a push to get me out of the tiny space we're presently sharing.

I draw in a breath and walk into the hallway. He joins me and motions to the left. A short walk later, we're at our door, and he swipes the key. I enter the room first and while it's a nice hotel, our room is small, so small we will be on top of each other every second we're here.

We set our bags down in the entryway and I walk to the other side of the room. By the time I turn around, Luke has followed me, only he stops shy of the window where I now stand, leaning on the desk that sits even with the foot of the bed.

The bed. I'm hyper-aware of it because it's the only place to sleep. Because I haven't been in a bed with him in two years. Because I don't know how to be in this room with him and not lose my mind.

He dials Adam on speaker. "You all cozy and comfy in your room?" Adam asks when he answers.

"You won't believe how cozy," I reply, "considering we hate each other."

Luke's eyes find mine, an intense burn in their depths that I'm too emotional to read properly. "Yes," Luke says. "We're all kinds of wonderful."

Adam makes it clear that he isn't sympathetic. "I bet it's better than being trapped in a car with Savage, telling stupid jokes with his shoes off."

And we're clearly on speakerphone on Adam's end as well, as Savage chimes in. "You dirty, dirty sinner you, Lucifer. Sleeping with the enemy."

"Oh my God," I murmur. "Can I punch him when I see him again?"

"As long as you don't shoot me, darlin'," Savage replies.

I walked right into that one, but I refuse to retreat. "A knee seems even better," I reply.

"He's a dick," Luke comments dryly. "But a loyal dick."

"Loyal dicks are the best dicks," Savage assures me.

"Please save me from this conversation," I plead, meeting Luke's stare. "Please."

A familiar, deep, sexy laugh rumbles from his chest. God, how I love his laugh. "There's no saving any of us from Savage," he assures me.

"And I'm in a car with him," Adam replies. "Did I mention he has his shoes off? Put your damn shoes on, man." I can almost hear Adam's scowl as he says, "We'd better have this conversation before I can't breathe anymore. We're still in Denver. We dropped Darius at the FBI offices. He didn't go home when he left. He's currently at the Ritz Carlton, which is nine hundred dollars tonight for the smallest room. I get him wanting to stay away from his home, but this feels extravagant for an FBI agent that isn't making money on the side."

"Agreed," I say, and little things about Darius's behavior over time niggle at me now as I add, "We both make a decent living, not a nine-hundred dollar a night Ritz Carlton, decent though."

"That's what I wanted to know," Adam replies. "As it stands, we managed to get a room in the same hotel, and thanks to Blake, we're monitoring him through the hotel cameras. So far he's had no visitors. It's after noon now, and he hasn't gone to work. Blake hacked his schedule. He's due in at four."

My eyes go to Luke's. "How did he hack the schedule?"

"Blake's a world-class hacker, sweetheart, but I doubt he went into the government system. It was probably on Darius's phone. Do you expect him to go to work after what happened last night?"

"Unless he walked into the agency and told them nothing, then he'll follow a protocol. He's FBI. We don't have the luxury of hiding from danger, but we also can't needlessly risk other people's lives. The challenge is that we don't know what he's told the agency, if anything. I'm missing. Do they know that? Maybe Darius is playing the same game we are, and trying to say very little, until he knows who he can trust. The best way for me to find out is for me to call Darius and my boss so we can compare their stories. But if I don't show up to my shift, all bets are off. I'm going to have to call my boss and tell him something. Otherwise, he's going to send out notifications of a missing agent."

"Wait to call Darius until we have a camera pointed at him," Adam suggests. "If he's dirty, he's going to call someone with that information. We need to know who he calls and on what phone. I'll let you know when."

"She'll call her boss when we hang up and we'll update you," Luke says. "What else?"

"Don't do anything stupid, Luce," Adam warns, and I'm not sure, but I think he means with me.

As if confirming my suspicion, Luke replies with, "I already did," before he adds, "Later, man," and disconnects.

He offers me his phone. "We'll get you a new phone in Breckinridge. One that will scramble your number and location."

I take a few steps and accept the phone, sitting down on the end of the bed, which is actually a whole lot closer to Luke than I intend. "What's our plan here? What do I tell my boss? What are your thoughts?"

It's a moment of déjà vu that tightens my throat. I used to tell him about my cases, and ask him that exact question. He feels it, too. I see it in the tightening of his lips and his heavy pause before he says, "My opinion," he glances over at me, "is to tell him the truth. You were attacked. You're hiding. Ask about Darius. Show concern. Is Mike still your direct supervisor?"

"He is."

"Well, you've always questioned Mike's decision-making. I wouldn't stop now."

I'm reminded of one of the sexiest things about Luke Remington. He offers commands when we're naked and debate when we have our clothes on. Not the best thought to have while sitting on a bed in a hotel room with him. Which is why I refocus on the topic at hand, which is Mike. He's not wrong about him. Mike has been a source of frustration to me when it comes to my job growth. He could push to allow me to grow right here in Colorado. He just doesn't. I suddenly wonder if there's a reason beyond him generally being a jerk. Which is ridiculous. This mess I'm in can't be connected to my personal and professional life.

Can it?

"Let's hope I get his voicemail," I say, before punching in his number.

After a few rings, bingo. Voicemail. I shake my head to let Luke know and then wait for the beep. On my cue, I say, "Mike, it's Ana. I'm safe. I'm on a hitlist, as is everyone in my small circle. I don't know if it's personal or professional, so be careful. I'll call you when I can do so safely." I disconnect and hand Luke his phone.

He immediately shoots off a text before saying, "I let Adam know what just went down. He'll watch for any electronic trail chain reaction involving Darius." He pushes off the desk and stands, towering over me, and when I say the room is small, it's *small*. His legs are all but touching my legs. My breath catches in my chest and I steel myself for the impact of our always intense connection, as I tilt my chin up to meet his stare. I find him staring down at me, his eyes half-veiled, tension in his jaw, in his body. God, in *my body*.

When I think I can't take the silence anymore, I say, "Luke—"

"I'll go shower so you can have the bathroom as long as you want." That's it. That's all he says before he moves away from me and walks across the room, grabs his bag, and disappears into the bathroom, shutting the door.

CHAPTER TWENTY-FIVE

Lucifer

Holy hell. Ana and the damn tiny hotel room are going to be the death of me.

I lean on the bathroom door, running a rough hand over the two-day-old stubble on my jaw. She keeps looking at me with those big, beautiful eyes filled with regret and guilt, but I'm not sure if that guilt's about shooting me or wanting the man who killed her brother. Probably both, which translates to exactly where we already were before now. She will always hate me. I'd be a fool to forget that fact.

I yank my shirt over my head, pull the tie from my hair, and crank up the shower, but I don't plan to suffer in the cold water. I'm hot and hard, but not even an ice bath is going to fix that when Ana alternates those guilty looks with lusty stares that make me want to undress her. Okay, everything makes me want to undress her. She's Ana, and for me, no one else compares. I put that to the test these past two years and proved it accurate. No matter how hot the woman, how sweet the woman, how perfect a woman seemed, no one else was Ana.

And it's damn sure bittersweet right about now.

I step under the spray of the shower and let the water work on the tension in my shoulders, my mind chasing memories. The moment that bullet hit my gut and I'd gone down. I'd blacked out and come to with Ana leaning over me.

"I got you," she'd said. "The ambulance is on the way. Can you hear me, Luke?" She'd patted my face. "You're going to be okay."

Talk about confusing as fuck, considering she's the one who shot me. I'd faded in and out of consciousness. I'd heard "training accident" somehow, so when the hospital asked me what happened, that's what I said. But I already knew the truth.

Flash forward a few hours later—or hell, maybe it was longer than that—and I opened my eyes to feel someone watching me. I glanced around, my eyes landing on the glass window, where I'd found Ana standing, tears streaming down her cheeks. But she didn't come in. I didn't see her again. I don't think she was crying because I almost died. Maybe it was the guilt over wanting me dead.

Days later, I still don't know how many, I hadn't seen Ana since that window incident, but Jake told me what he'd said to the police. Kasey was killed by hostiles, and we managed to bring his body back with us. I expected Trevor to tell a different story to save his ass and turn Ana against me. It shouldn't have worked. Not even for a moment.

It was Jake who told me the details of Kasey's funeral. I wasn't even supposed to be out of bed that day, but I checked myself out despite the protests of the nurses. I didn't go to the church. I'm not that much of a hypocrite. But I went to the cemetery.

I press my hands to my face with the memory. Fuck, fuck, fuck. Kasey was family, until he wasn't. And Ana was still the woman I loved.

It was snowing that day and so damn cold. I stood behind a tree and watched the ceremony, watched Ana's body quake with tears that I was on some level responsible for creating. I had no choice but to kill

Kasey, but I was still the man who pulled that trigger. As the guests slowly faded from the scene, Ana was the last person there that day. Her body quaked and her pain reached across the divide between us and bled right into me.

I needed to comfort her.

Only then did I step out from behind the tree, but my feet froze on the icy ground as I reminded myself that she shot me. She blamed me. She hates me. Some things about these memories are past tense. Some are both past and present. I have no idea why she even saved me from prosecution. Her gaze had lifted and she'd stared at me from a distance, and then she turned and walked away, her hate for everything to do with me crystal clear.

I turn off the water, and thank God for memories that remind me that she didn't even hear my story. I'd walked in the door of The Ranch's main living quarters. I grab the towel, seeing her tear-streaked face, hearing the words, she said to me at some point in that confrontation—I don't even remember exactly when. "You bastard," she'd hissed. "You killed him." And that's it. I'm done with this trip down memory lane.

I wrap the towel around me and for the good of both me and Ana, I grab my phone, turning on some good old classic rock n' roll, AC/DC's "Back in Black" and sing along. I pull on a pair of sweats I bought at the store for the drive, and don't bother with a shirt. I dry my hair though—that shit is long—and the longer I'm in the bathroom, the better for me and Ana.

When I can stall no more, I decide I'll give her the bathroom and go on to sleep while she's in here. Then I don't have to think about the bed and her in it naked, if at least one part of my body that is not my brain had its way.

Anger is burning in my belly, a product of a past I was thrown into, and the woman who lived, and in some ways died, inside that history with me. I open the door. Ana's sitting on the edge of the bed, staring at the door. The instant she sees me, her lips part, and her eyes travel my body before jerking back to my face.

"You have to put a shirt on. You just—*have to*."

My cock is pretty damn pleased with this reaction that says she wants me, but my brain is working overdrive, and for once, overpowering that plaything in my pants. "Why, sweetheart? You want to kiss the scar you gave me better? It's too late for that. Or maybe, you want to lick me all over? You already did that. You don't get to do it again. Not after trying to kill me." I walk to the end of the desk where I left my gun, pick it up, and then lay down on the ground at the foot of the bed. My phone goes to the floor. The gun sits on my gut.

Ana moves to the end of the bed, and sits there, staring down at me. "What are you doing?"

I notice she avoids my name when she would normally do otherwise. I guess she just can't figure out who I am anymore. Well, I know. And Lucifer fits. She knows, too. "I'm catching a few z's, and protecting you from anyone that comes in the door. If it so much as jiggles, I'll sit up and shoot."

"It's been a hellish night and morning. Lay on the bed. You can have the side closest to the door. Please."

I glance up at her. "Sweetheart, if I get in that bed with you, I'll have you naked in about thirty seconds, and while we'll both enjoy that, you'll just hate me for it after. Not to mention we won't get any sleep."

"I could say a lot of things to that response, but I probably shouldn't. We'll put pillows between us."

"If you think a pillow will stop me from getting naked with you, you might have been right when you said you never really knew me, Ana. That was right before you shot me, right? I told you. I want to fuck you. I don't want to sleep next to you."

She buries her face in her hands and groans a frustrating sound and then glowers at me, all sexy and way too damn hot for my own good. "Fine, *Lucifer*. Sleep on the damn floor. Just do what you want." She stands up and walks to the side of the bed before climbing on top.

She tosses a pillow down on top of me. I grab it and stick it under my head. "For the record, me down here and you up there is not what I want. It was never what I wanted, Ana. It's just who we are now."

"Yeah," she says softly. "I know. "

That's all she says and I want more. But then, I've always wanted more when it comes to Ana. And more was never enough.

CHAPTER TWENTY-SIX

Ana

My body is tired. My mind is tired. I need sleep, but I can barely breathe in this hotel room with Luke on the floor and me in this bed. I push off the mattress and grab my bag before walking into the bathroom and shutting the door. Once I'm inside the bathroom, I lean on the door, trying to find the energy to get in the shower, despite the fact that washing off the grime will feel heavenly.

I just don't know how to be with Luke, how to act, how to function when he's close. And yet if the last two years have proven anything, it's that I have never gotten comfortable with being without him, either. And the truth is that every moment I'm with him drives home how empty life has been without him. And yet, we're together and he's on the floor. His words play in my head: *I told you. I want to fuck you. I don't want to sleep next to you.*

I earned that attitude with a bullet. No, I earned it by standing against him, not with him. I force myself off the door and turn on the shower. Once I've peeled away my clothes, I step under the spray.

Instantly, I'm back in time, and not to the bad places I've lived most of the past two years, either. I'm in a good place, remembering that enchanting time in life when Luke and I were just finding each other. The night I'd agreed to have dinner with him. It was snowing, really snowing, but I knew soldiers and I knew them well. If he wanted to see me, no storm was going to keep him away. And he'd showed up with flowers and a bottle of champagne. And good Lord, in a snug T-shirt and jeans and a biker jacket, he'd looked sinful enough to earn his nickname, Lucifer. And he'd looked me up and down, in my own jeans and sweater, and then fixed me in a hungry stare that had my heart racing and sex clenching.

I wanted him.

I still do.

I slide back into that memory, reliving it.

I take the flowers from him, and say, "Come in. It's cold outside."

He enters the foyer, kicks the door shut, and with the champagne in his hand and the flowers in mine, he steps into me, cups my head and kisses me. Not a peck on the lips, either. He goes all-in with a deep slide of his tongue, all but claims me right then and there. Actually, I think he did that back at the coffee shop before I ever agreed to this date.

When his lips had parted from mine, he murmured, "I couldn't help myself. I kept thinking about kissing you again all day. I brought my truck. It'll plow right through the storm."

"I know a place that will deliver pizza no matter how bad the weather. You want to just stay in?"

"I can't promise I'll behave appropriately alone with you."

"I'm Kurt's stepdaughter. If you think I can't handle you, you've misjudged me."

He laughs this low, sexy laugh I feel in every part of me and says, "I found that out when you put me on my knees the first time I met you."

I blink back to the present and turn off the water. This isn't helping me deal with being this close to Luke. I force myself to blank out my mind, and I know that's why Luke cranked up the music when he showered. It's as Kurt taught us: don't leave room in your mind for anything but what is healthy for you right in the moment.

I pull on a pair of leggings, a long-sleeved T-shirt, and warm socks. I have a jacket I bought at the store, or I guess Blake bought, and I'll use it to cover my holstered weapon, but for now, I lay it on the tub. After which, I rush through drying my long blonde hair as much as anyone can do such a thing. I bought a little make-up at the store, simply because, when you feel normal, you act normal. Another trick Kurt taught all of his trainees. Not to mention, I'm with Luke.

Enough said.

I draw a deep breath and open the bathroom door. Luke is, of course, still on the floor, and I hope asleep. I resist the temptation to check on Luke—I mean, he might think I'm going for his gun—and instead climb onto the bed. I don't get under the covers. I just curl up and realize that my gun is on the nightstand.

That's how little I am afraid of Luke.

I left my gun behind when I went into the bathroom.

And shouldn't I be afraid of the man who killed my brother?

CHAPTER TWENTY-SEVEN

Lucifer

My alarm vibrates and I open my eyes, aware of my weapon on my belly, aware of Ana in the bed even without looking at her. I turn off the alarm, slide my phone into my pocket, and then push to my feet before setting my Glock on the desk. I expect Ana to be moving about with me, but instead, I find her curled up on her side, her own weapon on the nightstand within reach, and she doesn't budge. She's exhausted and I know her well enough to know she feels safe, or she'd be more alert. I'm not sure what to do with that information.

I walk to the side of the bed and sit down next to her and still, she doesn't react. "Ana," I say softly, and now she responds. She reaches for her weapon and sits up. I catch her wrist, keeping the weapon pointed at the ceiling.

"Oh God. I'm sorry," she says. "I'm so sorry. It's instinct. I was so dead asleep and we were being chased. I wasn't going to—"

"I know," I reply tightly, still remembering another time, another gun, and we both know it. "I know." I reach for her Sig, always her gun of choice, and she releases it into my palm. I set it on the nightstand and my palm comes down on her knee. "I didn't think you were going to shoot me."

Her hand goes to my arm and her touch is fire. Holy hell, how can I want someone who treated me like a criminal?

"Luke," she says, sounding breathless, "we need to talk about what happened."

I cup her face and drag her closer. "Talking isn't what I have on my mind right now. Do you have a problem with that?"

"I want to talk."

"Then you'd rather me not kiss you, I assume?"

"That's not what I said."

"That's good enough for me," I say, and my mouth slants over her mouth. My fingers splay between her shoulder blades, pressing her breasts to my chest, the feel of her, all woman—my woman, at one point, *mine*. And I can feel that possessiveness in me, that need to prove to her that she still wants me, she still loves me. I should just leave her alone.

But I can't.

She's proven that and proven it well.

My hand presses under her T-shirt, warm soft skin against my palm, and when I would start undressing her, my cellphone rings. I curse under my breath, hot and hard, frustration in my voice as I murmur, "Saved by the bell yet again."

I release Ana and pull my phone from my pocket to eye Adam's number, trying to ignore my raging hard-on that isn't going to be ignored. Still, I manage to answer with a tightly spoken, "Yeah, man."

"I need Ana to call Darius in about five minutes. He's waiting for a table in the hotel restaurant. We've got a tap on his line and a visual. We'll know if he uses another phone to contact someone after her call."

"Got it." I disconnect and hand Ana the phone.

"You need to call Darius in five." I stand and glance at my watch. "It's already getting late. I want on and off those roads to Breckinridge before nightfall. Let's get ready to leave once you make the call."

Ana nods and stands up and we both move around the hotel room as if nothing just happened, but something just happened. And we both know it's going to happen again.

CHAPTER TWENTY-EIGHT

Ava

There's really no time to think about what just happened between me and Luke.

We quickly gather the few things we have in the room, finish dressing, and prepare to leave the minute I'm off the phone. Still, the very act of doing things together—him and me, me and him, a pair, if not a couple—is surreal.

I've just slipped my jacket over my holster, and Luke has done the same when his cellphone buzzes with a text. He glances down at it, the stubble on his jaw now a heavy, several-day shadow, his long hair not as long as when I met him. It's now to his chin, and I like it this way. Not that what I like matters.

"It's time," he says, handing me the phone.

I accept it, the brush of our fingers creating a collision of our stares, and while we might not have time to think or talk about what just happened, it's here between us, heavy and wild, a storm that is brewing, rather than a storm that has passed. "What should I tell him?"

"Use your instincts, Agent."

I draw a breath and exhale as I sit. "What number will come up on his caller ID?"

"A random location. A random number. He won't be able to call you back. Tell him you borrowed a stranger's phone."

I don't ask how Walker can do this and the FBI doesn't do it for our agents. It doesn't matter right now. I dial Darius and wait for an answer, not sure he'll take the call, considering he doesn't know the number. Then again, I'm missing. He'll take the call. He proves me right on the second ring. "Agent Sanchez."

"Darius, it's me."

"Ana. Ana, shit. Where are you? Are you okay? I've been worried as hell."

"I'm Teflon. You know that. I'm good. I got away, but I'm staying away until I figure out what this is about."

"What about Luke? Is he with you?"

"No." My eyes meet Luke's as I say, "I left Luke back at the house. I don't know who to trust. What about you? Are you okay?"

"Yeah. Those goons of Luke's dropped me at the FBI office. I'm in a hotel. I'm not going home. Mike doesn't want me at the office until we find out what we're dealing with. Do you know?"

"There's a hitlist and I'm on it. I think you were just unlucky enough to be with me."

"A hitlist? No shit. Do you know who's on it? Do you know who's behind it?"

There's something in his voice that doesn't sit well. "No," I say. "I know nothing right now, but my godfather is dead. I went to Estes Park before I got on a plane and got the hell out of Colorado."

"Jake is dead?"

"Yeah, Darius, he is. And his daughter is pregnant. Her husband died a month ago in an accident. It's not a pretty picture."

"What do you know that someone doesn't want you to know?"

"That's just it," I say. "I don't know anything. I have no idea what this is about. None. I haven't been involved in anything Jake or Luke was involved in for years. It makes no sense."

"Does Luke have answers?"

Asking a question again, in another way, means he doesn't believe what I'm telling him. "I don't have any idea," I say. "If you find him, ask him. I ditched him. Remember?"

"Yeah, well, someone wiped the cameras for miles near my place. I can't get Luke, his buddies, or you on camera. We dropped a lot of bodies at my place. I'm working on identifying them. No ID on any of them yet. Maybe their names will help. How can I call you back?" I can almost hear him frowning. "Caller ID said you're in Utah."

"I'm moving around," I say. "And I borrowed some lady's phone. I need to go. I'll call you when I can. I'm chasing a lead."

"Tell me what it is and I'll help."

"Too dangerous. Stay safe." I disconnect and stand up, handing Luke the phone. "He seemed off. I don't like how that call felt, but if he's dirty, he's also the only path to answers we have. At some point, we'll have to decide how I use my relationship with him to get answers."

"Don't underestimate Adam and Savage. They're watching him. Let's get out of here. We have an SUV waiting on us downstairs, with the keys under the seat." I nod and we both grab our bags and head for the door. Our stay in the hotel room is over. And somehow, we both kept our clothes on.

These are not the good old days. Not even close.

CHAPTER TWENTY-NINE

Ana

From the moment Luke and I step out of the room, we're both on guard, cautiously analyzing our surroundings. Once we're inside a shiny black SUV that looks and smells new, Luke's phone rings. "Adam," he answers on speaker. "You're on with me and Ana."

"He called Mike, and had the conversation you'd expect. Worry for you, Ana, and yadda, yadda, yadda. But what was interesting was that he then pulled out a throwaway phone and made another call. I was at the next table."

"He didn't recognize you?" I ask.

Luke answers. "He's the invisible man, sweetheart, a master of disguise. You'd be shocked at how well he can change his looks."

Sweetheart.

It means nothing except that old habits don't die easily, but I still notice. I still feel it in my belly. "What did you hear?" I ask.

"Nothing. The dirty bastard got up and walked away. But he's using a throwaway," Adam adds. "That looks dirty to me."

"Maybe," I say.

"*Maybe?*" Luke asks in disbelief.

"Probably," I amend. "But I'm not working his present case with him. I have no idea how that might play into whatever he's working on right now."

"I'll get Blake to find out what's he's working on," Adam replies, "but the man wears Snoopy socks. I don't trust him."

I laugh. "He must be working a case. He doesn't wear Snoopy socks. I'd have noticed."

Adam grunts. "He's on the move. I need to go." He hangs up.

"I thought you two were partners?"

"Not since I started profiling."

"Then why were you at his place?"

"He wanted some advice on a case." I glance over at him. "Maybe he just wanted to get me there. I just don't want to believe that."

"Of course not," he says flatly. "You've been friends so long. Why would you jump to conclusions?"

The words jab at me and I say, "Luke."

He turns on the radio and shifts into gear, setting us in motion. I want to turn the radio down and tell him I'd only found out Kasey was dead minutes before he arrived. I was in shock. I was grieving. I was not in my right mind. I want to tell him it was an accident. I want to tell him I still love him.

But he doesn't want to hear anything I have to say.

This is going to be a long drive to Breckenridge.

CHAPTER THIRTY

Ana

The ride to Breckenridge is a scenic two hours with decent two-lane roads, unless you get detoured for high winds, which is more common than anyone hopes for. Thankfully we are not detoured, but the winds are nevertheless crazy high and intense. So is the silence between me and Luke that is filled with classic rock, which Kurt always loved. I can barely take the silence, and I try to focus on the songs, on the words, and I know he is as well.

I even think that's a good thing, until it's not. We lose the channel and I work the knob to find another station. The dial lands on a country station, which works for both of us. Usually. Maybe not so much today. The first song that starts playing is Dustin Lynch's "Love Me or Leave Me Alone." The words: *So love me or leave me alone Hold me or just let me go,* don't exactly set the tone we're going for right now, and I don't miss the way Luke's fingers curl around the steering wheel. I reach over and flip the channel again, and leave it on some DJ talking to another DJ. It's a good plan, but I'm back to, until it's not. This is apparently another country station. Carly Pearce's "Every Little Thing" begins to play and my stomach knots. I haven't been able to listen to this song since Luke and I split up.

Every little thing
I remember every little thing
The high, the hurt, the shine, the sting

Luke starts driving faster. I draw a deep breath as he slides in between two cars and tails the one in front of us so closely that they move to the next lane. We're now at the part of the drive where there are steep drops to our left, drops *without* rails—long, deep, dangerous drops that go on and on forever, and ensure certain death should you tumble off the road.

I'm afraid of heights.

I don't know why, and Kurt tried everything he could to get me past it, but nothing worked. Luke knows this secret about me but I don't think he's trying to scare me. This is his outlet—fast cars and motorcycles replaced his jets when he left the military. When he left the daredevil pilot side nicknamed "Lucifer" behind.

My fingers curl on my lap, and I force myself to draw in a breath. The damn song keeps playing.

Guess you forgot what you told me
Because you left my heart on the floor

Luke speeds up yet again. I squeeze my eyes shut, force myself not to look at the road or the steep drop. If we die, we die together. It would be a fitting end to us both, I guess. I'm not sure why it's fitting. I can't think straight right now in order to put that into an articulate thought. The song ends and Garth Brooks' "Friends in Low Places" comes on. I sing the lyrics in my head, blocking out everything else. I lose time. I don't lose my anxiety. Luke finally slows down and I open my eyes but I don't look at him. Anger burns in my belly, sudden and fierce. Who am I kidding? I shot him. Of course, he was trying to scare me.

We're on the outskirts of Breckenridge now and I spy a store. "Please stop. I need to go the bathroom," I say, still not looking at him. *I need out of the truck*, I think. I need air. I need away from him.

He pulls over and parks at the far end of the store's lot. I open the door before he's even killed the engine, and I'm out, welcoming the brisk Colorado air. I fully intend to avoid Luke and get inside before him but that doesn't happen. As if he's jet fuel, he's in front of me, blocking my path. "I can't get you to feel shit now, can I? Not even fear."

My anger bubbles over. "You scared the shit out of me, asshole," I hiss, and try to slap him.

He catches my wrist. "You got away with that once, sweetheart. You don't get to do it again."

Sweetheart isn't so sweet right about now. "I could do it again if I really wanted to, and you know it."

"You could try."

"Let me go, *Lucifer*."

"Make me."

"You know I can. We've trained together. You didn't always win."

"Maybe I let you win."

"Let go," I say softly, not about to fight with him in a parking lot.

But he doesn't let me go. He pulls me closer, aligns our bodies so ridiculously close that I can feel how hard he is all over, *everywhere*. "What are you doing?" I demand.

"This," he says, his fingers tangling in my hair, his mouth slanting over my mouth, intensely demanding.

His tongue licks into my mouth with a long, seductive, commanding swipe, and then another that consumes me and the anger I try desperately to hold onto. This is a game to him, one meant to punish me, one that's about control—his and not mine—and he's winning. I want to push him away. I want to shout at him to stop this back and forth and all the torment that

135

comes with it. But he proves all too easily that I have no resistance where he's concerned.

I'm without the will to fight him, weak, so ridiculously weak where Luke is concerned. As always with this man, he demands and I demand more, not less. In my mind, I want to fight him, I want to fight *with* him, I want to push him to talk. Instead, I am instantly desperate for more of him, my body pliable, wet, aching. I want to be back in the hotel, stripping him naked and punishing him for hating me, even if it's me that deserves the punishment.

Fine.

He wants to play this game, I'll play. I melt into him, kiss him back, my hands stroking up his back, over his body. As if he senses the change in me, as if he fears I'll be in control, not him, he pulls back, lips lingering above mine, our breathing heavy, labored. "Damn you, woman," he murmurs, and then he releases me, quickly putting space between us.

He leans against the truck, hands on his hips, a lift of his chin as he says. "Go to the bathroom so we can get back on the road."

He didn't win. I'm just not sure I won, either. I'm not sure there is a way for either of us to win, and I'm not sure what that means. I walk toward the store, my lips swollen, every part of me humming from his touch. I need that bathroom, and I pray it's the small, one-stall spot that I can use to pull myself together.

Thankfully my wish proves reality. I step into the small bathroom, lock the door and stare at myself in the mirror. The truth is that I don't like the woman looking back at me right now. Neither does Luke. And there's nothing I can do to fix either of those things. Nor do I have time to dwell on any of this. I wash up and open the door to find Luke leaning on the wall.

He doesn't straighten and I step closer to him, which I could pretend is to battle eye-to-eye, but I don't want to battle with him anymore. Still, the words that come out of my mouth are combative. "Afraid I'll run?"

"No, Ana. Just making sure you're safe."

"You know I can protect myself."

Now he stands, towering over me. "You'd be dead right now if it weren't for me."

He's right. So very right, and I quickly say as much. "I would be dead without you. There's no question about it. You saved my life. Thank you. I'm surprised you cared enough to come for me."

"I would never let anyone hurt you, Ana. Ever." His voice is a bit gravelly, hinting at emotion he may not want to allow to surface.

I know this because I feel it too, the pinch in my chest, the pull at my heartstrings. We're familiar, and in a good way. "I don't like how all the hate between us feels."

"Me either," he replies. "But it lives on, a scar from a blade that cut too deep." He doesn't give me time to reply. "Let's get out of here."

I nod and he follows me out of the store. Once we're outside, we walk side-by-side toward the SUV. Together. But not together at all.

CHAPTER THIRTY-ONE

Lucifer

I can still smell her on my skin. What the hell is this woman doing to me?

We can't get to the Walker house in Breckinridge soon enough for me, and thank *fuck,* it's about seven thousand square feet of breathing room. But it takes fifteen minutes that feel like an hour to travel the back roads that lead to the private property nestled in between mountains and trees.

"Holy wow," Ana murmurs as she takes in the modern home that's wood, glass, and stone, with a bit of a Jenga stackable block thing going on. "It puts The Ranch to shame."

"The Walker team doesn't do anything in a little way." I idle in the driveway and call Blake. "We're here," I say when he answers.

The doors to the garage immediately open. "Savage and Adam are on the way to you now. I sent Dexter, Smith, and Wyatt to watch Darius and do some digging around. They got there early this morning."

I pull into the garage. "That's a lot of firepower. I don't want to pull them off other things."

"That's not enough when one of our own is on the line," he says. "But it's a start. Get tucked in and cozy and call me."

"Check that, boss," I say and disconnect, as the garage closes behind us, obviously at Blake's hand.

"Savage and Adam are on the way here. We have a team in place monitoring Darius and offering support."

"Walker takes care of you," she says softly.

I glance over at her. "And you, Ana. One thing you are not right now is alone."

She swallows hard and nods. "That's nice to know," she says, but she reaches for the door and exits the truck.

Damn it to hell, can this thing between us be any more fucked up? I exit my side of the vehicle and grab both of our bags. Ana opens the door for me and we walk into the kitchen-living room combo with light wood and beams on the ceiling, a fireplace, and killer views. I set our bags on the table right next to a long island. "We'll be able to load up on supplies, including firepower before we leave."

"I need to go back and corner Darius. I can make him talk."

I don't remind her he most likely set her up to die. No good comes from that, not right now. "Let's see what Blake's dug up for us and we can chat it out. I'm not sure which room has clothes that work for you, but feel free to look around. The less time we're in public, the safer we are." I walk to the fridge and pull out a bottle of water, offering it to Ana.

She joins me on this side of the island and accepts it. I snag another for myself and down the cold beverage. It seems I'm perpetually hot as fuck and it started when I saw Ana again. When I set the bottle down, she's just looking at me.

"What is it, Ana?"

She studies me a moment, and then says, "Nothing now. I'll go find a room and think through what's going on here."

She starts to move away and I don't mean to, but I catch her arm and pull her around to me. But I don't say anything. I don't kiss her again, but I sure as hell want to do that and more.

"Luke?" she prods softly when I say nothing.

"We'll stay through morning. We can talk about what comes next after Savage and Adam get here."

"Right. Okay."

Still, I don't release her, but I have to. I know I have to. My hand eases from her arm. Her eyes find mine, gorgeous eyes, eyes that have always told a story, and they did the night she shot me. She was hurting. She was filled with rage and anger.

Now, they're filled with regret, guilt, pain. The problem is none of those things change anything for either of us. Ana turns away from me and I let her go. But damn it, I don't want to.

CHAPTER THIRTY-TWO

Ana

I leave Luke standing in the kitchen and walk toward the dark wood staircase. I can feel his eyes on me. There is so much between us undone, unfinished, just plain not right, and so much I need to share with him, but just the idea of telling him what I now know about my brother feels like fuel to feed an explosion.

For now, I just need to get away and think, but I'm not sure if I should go up or down, since the house seems to be on several levels. I decide up is the most logical for bedrooms and after inspecting my room choices, soon I'm inside a fancy suite with mountain views and a full master bath that matches another room exactly. Inside the closet, I find clothes that seem as if they will work for me. What I don't have is a phone or a computer, and I really, really need to do some research.

Needing to feel in control, ready to run, to move, to fight, I head to the closet, kick off my boots and remove my jacket and weapon. I try on clothes and pack a week's worth of clothing before I head to the bathroom where I find a cabinet with a remarkable supply of toiletries, a flat iron, and a hairdryer. There are extras of everything. My God, Walker Security really is prepared for anything. I can only imagine what the weapons room looks like.

I've been in my room an hour and I can't stay here any longer. My stomach growls and I decide I'll hunt for food.

I pull my boots back on and slide my holster and weapon into place before I exit my room. The house is quiet, so very quiet, and I wonder if Luke is in one of what must be seven or so bedrooms sleeping, which is probably what I should be doing right now. I hurry downstairs to the kitchen, a little disappointed that I'm right and Luke is not present. After a little inspection of the pantry, I find boxes of mac n cheese. There's no milk or butter, but there are Ro-tel tomatoes. A little trick I discovered years ago is that a box of mac n cheese and Ro-tel whip up into a tasty meal.

Certain Adam and Savage will be here soon, and Luke has to be hungry, I put on the water in an extra-large pan, and proceed to cook a meal for an army. About the time the food is ready, the garage doors open, and when I would reach for my weapon for good measure, Savage's distinct cackle fills the air and I relax. I don't know what he thinks is funny, but anyone within ten miles probably does, too.

I grab several bowls, and as soon as Savage and Adam are in view, they're dumping their bags in the living room.

"Hi, honey, we're home," Savage says, stepping to the other side of the island. "What smells so good, chickadee?"

It's now, when I'm not fighting for my life, that I realize how tall and broad the man truly is. He's a beast. I'm not sure I made enough food.

"Spicy mac n cheese. Want a bowl?"

"I could eat the pan right now," he says, "but I'll take a bowl."

Adam steps to his side, and he's not all that much smaller, but there is a calmer demeanor about him. "Where's Lucifer?"

"You didn't kill him and bury the body this time, right?" Savage asks, accepting a bowl from me.

The joke, which isn't really that much of a joke, cuts. "Yes, I killed him and then made mac n cheese. That's how much of a bitch I am." I fill two bowls and slide one in front of Adam before offering them both forks and spoons, not sure which they will pick.

Adam's a fork guy. Savage is a spoon guy. I'm not surprised with Savage. I get the shovel it in and get back to killing kind of guy vibe from him.

I walk to the fridge and grab two beers and set them by their bowls.

"Hell yeah," Savage says, heading into the living room with his beer and bowl in hand.

Adam picks up his bowl and takes a bite, laughing. "Mexican mac n cheese. Damn good. Thanks, Ana." He grabs his beer and joins Savage.

Hoping for an update on what's going on, I grab a beer for myself and my bowl of mac and join them. "Any news on anything?"

"There's a couple of names on Luke's employee lists we can't reach."

"Who?"

"Dylan Black. Parker Conrad. Hayden Camden," Adam replies. "Dylan and Parker are in Texas. Hayden is in Knoxville, Tennessee."

Savage snorts. "Must be chasing ass. No one goes to Knoxville unless they're chasing ass."

Adam ignores him and adds, "We have men hunting for them now."

"They were all close to Luke," I say, more than a little concerned that those who are missing may be dead. "Does Luke know?"

"He knows," Adam confirms.

Then he's not sleeping, I think before I say, "Anything from anyone we did contact? What about Noah? He was close to Luke and I feel like those who were close are missing."

"We made contact with Noah," Adam confirms. "He's in Europe doing a contract job. He has no idea what's going on, but he knows to watch his back."

"And Darius?"

"We have men watching him," Savage says. "He doesn't act like a guy scared for his life. Just a guy hanging out and enjoying the Ritz." His bowl is empty and he points at mine. "You going to eat that?"

I hand him my bowl. "You only get that because you saved my life. And because there's more on the stove." I stand up and walk back to the kitchen, finding another bowl and filling it with pasta, eating where I stand, as I think about what I've learned. Those who Luke trusted the most, those who came to our house often as his friends, are the ones missing.

I finish off a bowl of mac, thinking about the list of people that Luke didn't trust. Once I've mentally compiled that list, I set my bowl in the sink and hurry back to the living room. "What about Carter?" I ask. "Did you talk to Carter?"

"Hold on," Adam says, setting his empty bowl on the coffee table. "Let me look at the list." He removes his cellphone from his pocket, punches a few buttons, and then says, "Yeah. Troy Carter is still in Denver. Blake talked to him. Why do you ask?"

"He was a pain in Luke's ass. It supports my theory that those who are missing were close to Luke."

"You seem to know Luke pretty well," Savage comments, kicking his feet up on the coffee table and crossing one ankle over the other.

"I was with him for four years."

146

"And you never thought he was dirty until you shot him?" Savage queries. "Explain to me how that works."

It's not a question. I glance at Adam, who is now sitting up straight, elbows on his knees, blue eyes pinned to my face, waiting on my reply to Savage's question. These two men are Luke's family. They don't see me as family at all. They see me as a potential enemy.

CHAPTER THIRTY-THREE

Ana

I don't cower when Savage confronts me. That's not the person Kurt raised. It's also not the woman Luke once loved. On that note, I could simply stand up and leave. I could tell Savage and Adam this is none of their business, but being an enemy amongst friends is not a space where I choose to live. They say the truth will set you free, but I work for the FBI. I also don't live in a fairytale. The truth can sometimes put you behind bars, or simply earn you the scorn of those around you.

But lies, lies are always a self-made prison and I choose the truth, no matter the outcome.

"It's not what it seems," I reply, which might not be the strongest start, but it's out there now, it's a launching pad.

"You shot him, darlin'," Savage replies dryly. "That's a simple fact."

"You did shoot him," Adam agrees. "That does indicate your desire to hurt him."

I wholly reject what I know appears obvious, but that's another thing my badge has taught me. The answers we seek are rarely as simple as they may seem. "No," I argue. "No, it does not. It was an accident."

Savage snorts. "We know who your stepfather was. We know how well he trained you. And we've seen you handle a gun. You don't shoot someone by accident."

I twist around to look at them more fully, to let them see the truth in my eyes. The eyes are always where you

149

find the real story. "I didn't think my brother was an angel, just the opposite. But you have to understand," I add, "I had one hero in my life and that was Luke. Kurt was a father figure, but he wasn't someone you could be human with. With Luke, I could and that never felt anything but safe."

"And yet, you shot him," Adam presses.

"No," I say.

"Yes," Savage counters.

"Just hear me out." I hold up my hands. "Trevor, one of the men that worked with Luke and Kasey, met me at my house, or rather, at The Ranch. Luke and I were both living there at the time." For a moment, I'm back in time as I open the door and find Trevor standing there.

"We need to talk," he says.

My heart had stopped. I'd been sure Luke and Kasey were both dead. "What is it? Where are they?"

He crowds me and pushes in through the front door and I let him, eager to hear what he's going to say. His hands are on my shoulders. "Kasey is dead. Luke shot him."

I blink in disbelief. "What?"

"You heard me. Kasey and a couple of the other guys are dead. Luke was running some illegal package and when Kasey busted him, he shot him and the others."

I blink the room back into view. "When he told me Luke had killed Kasey because Kasey caught him running an illegal package, I knew that wasn't true. That's not Luke."

"You knew your brother was a fucktard, but you shot Luke," Savage replies. "I might need a bottle of vodka for the rest of this story."

I feel the pressure to get my story out, but I keep my voice steady. I force myself to speak calmly when there might as well be an earthquake rumbling inside me right now. I've never told this story to anyone and it's emotional to get out. "I was shaking all over. I was angry with Luke. Couldn't he have shot him in the leg or the arm? I know what a master shot he is."

"You had to know that answer," Adam interjects. "You had to know Lucifer did what he had to do."

"Logically, yes, I don't disagree, but I had a human moment, despite how much those had been trained out of me. I didn't want to be logical. I wanted my brother to be alive. I wanted Kurt to be alive. I didn't want Luke, the man I love, to be the man who shot my brother."

"Go on," Adam urges softly.

"I made Trevor leave and when Luke showed up a few minutes later. I held a gun behind my back and my mind started going crazy. The minute I saw him and I felt all the familiar things you feel when someone you love comes home from the kind of missions he ran, I was scared. What if I loved him so much that I couldn't see the truth? I felt like I didn't know the man who would shoot Kasey dead. Which was unfair, because Kasey was always struggling in life. He was susceptible to trouble, but keep in mind, I'd lost Kurt the year before. I was a wreck. And Luke was my person in life. He's always been my one person, if that makes any sense?" I grab my beer and take a big slug.

"You said you didn't shoot Lucifer," Adam says. "What does that mean?"

"I pulled a gun on him, which was another mistake because I was trembling all over. I had no business holding a weapon, but nevertheless, I was, when suddenly Trevor was back inside the house, holding a gun on Luke, promising to kill him. Luke pulled his gun—and keep in mind he never pulled his gun on me—but he did on Trevor. When he turned to faceoff with Trevor, he hit my trembling hand holding the gun. I tried to catch it, afraid it would go off if it landed on the ground. Instead, when I caught it," I draw a breath, "it went off."

"Shit," Savage murmurs.

"I was angry with Luke," I say quickly, "even confused about why he would kill Kasey, but I didn't want him dead. I loved him. I still do. And Trevor was going to kill him. I saw it in his eyes. I grabbed my gun." I squeeze my eyes shut and for a moment I'm back there again, reliving that moment, holding my weapon on Trevor when I wanted to be on the ground, tending to Luke's wound. *I will kill you if you even think about shooting," I promise Trevor.*

"He deserves to die," Trevor snaps.

I blink Adam and Savage back into view, tears burning my eyes despite Kurt training me to never cry in public. "I shot his weapon out of his hand. I had no choice. I could see it in his eyes. He was going to kill Luke. I retrieved his weapon. He ran and I immediately called 911 and then went down on my knees and wrapped Luke's stomach."

"What happened to Trevor?" Adam asks.

"I never saw him again. A couple months later I discovered he'd been killed in a car accident not long after the funeral."

"What did the other men tell you about that day?" Adam asks.

"The only one who saw what went down was Jake. All he ever said was he had no choice. Three times he said it. Then he packed a bag and left."

"Did you ask for details?" Adam presses.

"I could barely catch my breath," I reply. "And the details didn't matter to me right then. Kasey was dead. I was looking at caskets, burying the brother my fiancé killed."

"You don't think it's odd that Jake hauled ass and left you at that point?" Adam asks. "Blake said from what he's dug up, he was Kurt's second for years."

"He was a father figure to me, but it ended up feeling like that best friend at work kind of thing. Once he was gone, he was pretty gone. And he was gone before that day and that mission. He had a chance to rekindle his relationship with his daughter that had gone south years before. He took it."

"What did you tell the police about any and all of this?" Savage asks.

"That it was a training accident," I say. "Luke backed my story when he woke up."

"Why didn't you explain this to Lucifer?" Adam asks.

"Again, repetitive here I know, but I was angry. I thought he knew. I still had to bury my brother. When I came back to reality, I tried to call him and his number was disconnected." They're both staring at me and I've hit my limit. "He won't believe me and I didn't tell the story to get you to tell him. I told you because you're offering me shelter and protection. You deserve to know that I'm not a crazy bitch who goes around shooting people I care about. That's not who I am. I would have stepped in front of a bullet for Luke and that includes the day I heard he killed Kasey. The truth is, I still would. But I'm human. I was hurt. I was angry. I felt betrayed by my hero. But I didn't want him dead."

"And yet, when you saw him for the first time in two years," Savage comments. "You seemed like you wanted him dead all over again."

"Yeah, well, I had two years to hate him for more than killing my brother. He left. I had two years to read into that all kinds of ways."

"In his reality, you shot him," Savage argues. "You made it clear you wanted him gone."

"I know. *I know*. But did he have to really go?" I hold up a hand again. "You don't have to say it. I don't pretend to be logical where Luke is concerned. The fine line between love and hate is real. And that's all. I'm going to my room to rest."

I stand up and Adam says, "I believe you."

"Me too, chickadee," Savage says solemnly. "I think you fucked it all up, but I also believe you love him."

A nod is all I can manage before I rush up the stairs. Adam and Savage believing me doesn't change the fact that Luke and I are where we are. I love him. I hate him. I love him all over again. And he feels the same. There's no turning back time.

CHAPTER THIRTY-FOUR

Lucifer

I heard every word Ana said to Adam and Savage.

I was on my way up the stairs after spending an hour in the armory that should have been fifteen minutes, if not for a call with Blake. I heard Ana's voice, and I stopped shy of the top of the steps, listening to her tell her story to Adam and Savage. I'm still on the stairs when Ana heads upstairs and hurries toward her room.

I don't follow, not yet. I need a damn minute. I climb the last few steps from the lower level and walk into the main room, ignoring Savage and Adam. Instead, I go to the liquor cabinet off the kitchen, grab a bottle of vodka, and down a few swallows, and while the burn is real, there is no burn quite like the burn that has been Ana on my life.

I down another slug and set the bottle down. I decide vodka is a bastard when it fails to drag me out of the past, and instead shoves me right back inside those memories. Back to the night Ana shot me and I squeeze my eyes shut, reliving it like it was yesterday...

I pull up to The Ranch, my home for the past year since Ana and I moved in, with the cloak of evening upon us now. I've delivered the princess to safety, but I've brought back body bags, one of which is Kasey's and now I have to tell Ana that I killed him. I park the SUV in the garage and kill the engine, running a hand over my face, trying to figure out how to tell her, and for about the hundredth time, I have no fucking clue.

Every way I come up with leads to the same place: her absolute torment and pain.

I sit there a good ten minutes, rethinking what happened. Could I have shot him and not killed him? And I get the same answer I always come up with: no. He was a skilled man with a gun in his hand, intent to kill in his mind and body, and a will to survive, not die. He would have killed the princess if I had left him alive. He would have killed me.

Either way, no matter what my answer, there's no putting off what has to happen right now. Ana deserves to know Kasey is gone.

I open the truck door, my weapon under my leather jacket. I hesitate a moment, thinking about this weapon being the weapon that killed Kasey. I consider removing it, but me without my gun would feel off to Ana. I walk toward the door, dread clawing at me, a wild animal ripping me apart from the inside out.

I reach for the doorknob to the kitchen and draw a breath, forcing myself to open it and just go inside. And isn't in the kitchen but when I walk into the living room I find her standing in the middle of the room, tears streaking her cheeks. Shit. She knows. How the hell does she know?

"You killed him?" she demands. "You killed Kasey?"

I close the space between me and her and when I'm standing in front of her, my hands come down on her shoulders. "He's dead. I'm so sorry, Ana."

"Did you kill him?"

"Ana—"

"Did you kill him?" she grinds out between her teeth.

"He killed three of our men. He had the princess I was guarding at gunpoint. It was me and her, or him."

"So, you killed him." This time it's not a question.

"Ana—"

"I never understood how love could turn to hate. Now I do." She moves her hand from behind her back and her gun presses to my belly. "Why? Why would you do this to me? He was my brother."

"Sweetheart—"

"Don't call me that. Don't. I'm not your anything anymore."

"I love you. I would never—"

"Liar!" she shouts, her voice and body quaking. "Liar! He's dead and you did it."

"Jake was there. He'll tell you—"

"Tell me about the package," she demands, a teardrop sliding down her cheek. "What package?"

"I don't know what it was or where it is. It disappeared at the same time as Trevor. He was working with Kasey. Put the gun down. You don't want to shoot me."

"What if I do?"

"We both know you don't."

Her shoulders tremble, as does her hand. She's barely holding onto the gun. I could take it from her, but I've already taken so much. "I love you," I repeat. "Can I have the gun and we'll get through this together?"

"Now I know why they call you Lucifer. It's not about your piloting skills. It's about killing. You're the devil."

I flinch with those words that hit a little too close to home. I have killed. In fact, I've killed more than my share of men. And I never thought twice about it either, not until I met Ana. My job, and the enemies I faced most of my career, made me callous and cold. She made me human. I'm not sure I'd ever explain that to her and make her understand.

There's a sound to my right and suddenly Trevor is there, holding a gun on me. "Time to die, you little prick."

I pull my weapon and turn away from Ana to face Trevor, that piece of shit that turned on us all. But I've barely turned when I feel the bullet rip through me. I can feel myself falling and I shoot toward Trevor, but I don't know if I hit him. Everything goes black. Then Ana's over me, fresh tears streaming down her cheeks. "I'm so sorry, Luke. I'm sorry. I didn't mean for this to happen."

I blink back to the present and find Adam standing next to me. "You heard?"

"I heard."

"What are you going to do about it?"

I pick up the vodka, take a slug and hand him the bottle before I step around him. In a few long strides, I'm charging up the stairs toward Ana's bedroom.

CHAPTER THIRTY-FIVE

Ana

Once I'm inside my bedroom, I strip away my holster and weapon and then I pace back and forth, counting every step, trying to control my thoughts. I have no phone. I have no music. Counting is the only way to keep myself from thinking of things I cannot change. Like the fact that Luke is in another room right now and I don't even know which one. I should go to him and say what? I accidentally shot him? He'll send me back to my room.

I'm pacing again when there's a knock on the door.

I suck in a breath, not sure what to expect. God, was someone else found dead? With dread, I walk to the door and open it, stunned to find Luke standing there. He's still in the clothes he wore when we arrived—jeans and a T-shirt, both of which hug his muscular, perfect body. A body that has known my body in every possible way. His gun and jacket have gone. His longish hair is mussed up, as if he's been running his fingers through it. As if he fretted about his decision to come here to my door.

"Luke?" I whisper tentatively, not sure what to expect.

The minute I say his name, he steps forward, his hands on my waist, his touch possessive, branding me, though it's far from necessary. I'm his. I've always been his. It seems nothing can change that. I can never belong to anyone else. Still, I have no idea why he's here. I back up, step out of his reach just enough for him to kick the door shut, but no more.

I don't want distance from Luke. I don't want to give him space one little bit. And he doesn't complain. Instead, he stands there a moment, a few inches between us, staring down at me, his blue eyes smoldering.

"A fine line between love and hate, right, sweetheart?" he asks, softly.

"You heard what I said."

"I heard."

"I didn't shoot you. The gun—"

"Fell. I heard it all."

He catches my hip and walks me into him, his hand sliding to my lower back, molding me closer.

"So, what is it right now, Ana?" His fingers find my hair, a rough, erotic pull to his grip as he drags my mouth near his. "Love or hate?"

It's a trick question when I can feel him hard against my belly. The familiar earthy scent of him seduces me, his warm breath fanning my lips, and I can almost taste his mouth on mine. In this moment, I both revel and loathe him as much as I do myself. He killed my brother, and I can't live without him. It's like a joke played on me by the universe. My fingers curl in his T-shirt, ball around the material as I whisper, "Both. I feel both."

"Right now," he says, "that's good enough." His mouth slants over mine, his tongue stroking long. I can taste his hunger and I wonder if he can taste mine. Because I *am* hungry for Luke, this man I once thought would be my husband.

I need him.

I need him so badly it's a physical pain.

I don't even try to find what is between us. I slide my hands under his shirt, the feel of his warm skin and hard abdominal muscles stirring that need inside me. He's still so deliciously male, damn him. I shove his shirt upward, and he pulls it over his head, tossing it away.

God, this is happening. It's been so long that I swear I'm trembling.

We're by the bed now and I don't even know how we got here. It's irrelevant. He's the only thing that matters to me right now. His shirt has barely hit the ground when my hands run up and down his sides, but he's focused on my shirt. It's gone before I can blink, and my bra with it. Somehow, I'm against the wall by the fireplace—again the room just keeps fading in and out— and his powerful legs are framing mine, his hungry stare raking over my breasts.

"God, you're still so damn beautiful," he murmurs.

I laugh, an aroused choked sound and point out the obvious. "You say that when you're looking at my breasts."

He cups them, teasing my nipples in that perfect way he does, his eyes on my face now. "Like I said: so fucking beautiful." His voice is low, rough, raw with emotion that I feel, too.

"Luke," I whisper, unable to find my voice.

His hand is back on my face, tilting my gaze to his. "Is there someone else? Are you seeing anyone?"

My lashes lower, my fears over him moving on real and present. "Ana," he presses.

I look at him. "No. I'm not. Are you?"

"I didn't date anyone. I'm not dating anyone. But I sure as hell fucked everyone I could fuck to try and forget you," he confesses. "It didn't work."

The idea of him with who knows how many women cuts deeply, but I try to force myself to think logically. I shot him, I almost killed him, I told him there was no us anymore. "Can you just kiss me and stop talking, please," I murmur, catching long strands of his hair with my fingers.

He cups my face and looks down at me. "I thought you were done with me. I would never—"

"I know," I whisper. "Believe me, I know. I handled everything horribly."

"You were grieving. I shouldn't have left you."

"I shot you, Luke, and despite the fact that it was an accident, I held the damn gun on you. We both know you never point a gun you aren't willing to shoot." My voice softens and my hand presses to his face. "I needed someone to blame. *I'm sorry.*"

"You needed comfort. I wasn't there." His lips thin and he releases me, hands on his hips as he stares at me. "Did you and Darius—"

"God no, no, no. You think I'm not strong enough to survive life without someone in my bed, Luke?" I try to move away from him and he catches my hand but I don't look at him.

"It was two years, Ana. I hate the idea of you with him or anyone else, but I know I left. I know—"

I turn to face him and try to cover my breasts with my free arm. "I didn't sleep with Darius. I didn't sleep with anyone, okay? Are you happy?"

"No one?"

"No one," I breathe out, embarrassed and I'm not sure why. I could have. I just didn't want to. "I just—I didn't."

He folds me into him and cups my face. "Because you're mine," he murmurs, but he doesn't give me the chance to confirm or deny that statement.

His mouth closes down on my mouth, and warmth seeps through my body. I moan with the taste of him, melt into the hard lines of his body and submit to all that I feel for Luke. And how can I not? This kiss is like none of the others we've shared since we've found each other again. That hunger is still there, but there is so many ways the kiss speaks what we have not said. There is love in this kiss, there is tenderness, there is the deep, rich wonderful history we have shared together. But deep in the depths of all that is wonderful, I remind myself that there is still pain, torment, and betrayal. We can't erase some parts of ourselves and keep only the parts we want to hold onto. Life just doesn't work that way.

When Luke parts our lips, he strokes a lock of hair behind my ear, a shiver running down my spine with that simple little touch. My reaction pretty much sums up why I wasn't with anyone else. Who would compare to Luke? Who could make me feel so good so easily? The answer is no one.

"Undress for me," he orders softly.

I laugh a bit shyly, which is silly. This is Luke. And Luke has always liked to watch me undress. "I'm pretty close to naked already."

"Half-naked. Undress for me," he repeats, his hands falling away from me as he sits down on the bed.

I know then, of course, that he wants to feel like us again, but it runs deeper than that, I think. He wants me to show him that I trust him. And I do. I trusted him so much that when I felt betrayed, my reaction was over the top. Maybe he shouldn't want my trust. Maybe my trust is dangerous.

But I'm not denying him what he's asking for. I'm not denying him anything, not tonight.

CHAPTER THIRTY-SIX

Lucifer

THE PAST...

I sit across from Ana on our first date at a popular upscale Italian restaurant, lit up inside and out by her soft voice, her beautiful smile, her luminous blue eyes. She is a deadly angel. A woman with the skills to kill you, and the sense not to if she can find another way. I have no idea why this appeals to me so much, aside from the obvious. She's a fucking beautiful badass and while some might be intimidated by her or the man she calls father, I am not.

I want her.

Should I walk away? Probably. Am I good enough for her? Probably not.

But then, I have never pretended to be the angel I believe her to be. Not with her or anyone. I am what I am. She can take me or leave me—it might be better for her own good if she left me—but I'm damn sure going to make certain she feels good in the process.

"Wine?"

"Yes, please. That sounds good."

"What do you prefer?"

"Red like roses, white is almost like water," she jokes. "I vote red."

"Any preferences?"

"Not too dry."

I glance at the menu and when the waiter stops by, I order an expensive bottle, riding the bonus lining my pocket for an independent contractor job that starts next week.

"You seem to really know your wine."

"I spent about two years in Italy and another two in France."

"Are you glad to be back here?"

"Now I am," I say, making it clear that I'm talking about her. And it's true. I'm fucking elated to be right here at this table with her. There is something about Ana that outshines every woman before her, and I've had my share as a young rowdy pilot, who perhaps had more of a God complex than the Lucifer title I earned. Now, I save the Lucifer comparison for reasons no one would understand.

"Do you have family, Luke?" she asks, really the only person other than Kurt who calls me Luke rather than Lucifer.

"My father was a pilot, which is why I became a pilot. He died in a combat situation. My mother died in a car accident a year later, just before I enlisted."

When others would apologize as if they were responsible for my parents' deaths, Ana studies me intensely, just studies me as if I'm a science project. The waiter arrives with our bottle of wine. When finally, our glasses are filled and Ana has approved of the wine, I say, "What are you thinking, Ana?"

"You defeat your demons by facing them, thus why you became a pilot. I admire that courage."

"Everyone else thought I was crazy for getting in a jet."

"I would argue you're not because you did." She doesn't give me time to reply. "My father died of a heart attack when I was quite young, too young to remember him. My mother also died in a car accident, but it wasn't an accident."

My spine stiffens. "Murdered?"

"Yes."

"Because of Kurt?"

"Yes."

"Did he make them pay?"

"He says he did," she confirms.

"Then he did," I assure her. "And then he raised you."

"Yes. Yes, he did."

We continue to talk throughout our meal. I barely taste the food though, for how much I want to taste her, and I don't hold back after I pay the bill. We exit the restaurant with her hand in mine, me holding onto her when I don't know that I've ever wanted to hold onto another woman. I just thought it wasn't in my blood. It's not like my mother and father had a shit relationship. He was just never home and she was always alone. It didn't feel like something worth wanting. A fast fuck did the job. That's not what I want with Ana.

We reach the truck and I don't walk her to the passenger side of the vehicle. I take her with me to mine and turn her to face me, sliding my hand under her hair to her neck. "I can't seem to help myself."

I close my mouth over hers, kissing her in the kind of slow, sensual way you savor the finest of wines. I'm hot. I'm hard. I'm intensely aware of the soft sound of submission she makes, as if she too has caved to the inevitable between us, and cannot resist its lure, at least in the moment. She melts into me, her arms wrapping around me, and when I say, "I want to take you home, Ana. I know you just met me, but—"

"I don't want to go home."

I kiss her again, this time fast and hard, the heat in my blood and the thickness of my cock against my zipper pressing me to get her home and do so now. My thumb strokes her cheek and then I help her into the truck.

***

I live in a high-rise apartment I rented the day I returned to the city to stay.

Ana and I walk through the lobby to the elevators. Once we're inside the empty car, I drag her to me and kiss her again, refusing to give her the time to feel or have second thoughts. I'm rewarded with another one of her sweet, sexy moans.

When our lips part, I say, "God, woman, I want my tongue all over your body."

Her lips part in surprise and when I would kiss her again, she presses her fingers to my lips. "I'm pretty sure they have cameras in here."

I capture her hand and remove it from my mouth. "Are you shy?"

"Private is more like it," she replies. "Do with me what you might, if I let you, but it's between you and me."

I like this answer. It's a line drawn in the sand and challenge—one I plan to rise to meet. The elevator dings and the doors begin to open.

"There are no cameras in the elevator," I tell her. "There should be, but there absolutely is not. And for the record, I like privacy as well and I hope like hell you *do* let me." I lace the fingers of one hand with hers and lead her out of the car, down the hallway, and to my apartment.

Once we're inside, I take her coat, kissing her shoulder as I do. She shivers under my touch, which pleases me. This deadly angel has a delicate side I'm obsessed with discovering more of. When she wants to. That's one of the hottest sides to Ana. It's easy to see that she chooses when to be rough and tough and when to be a delicate, blossoming flower, and with who. The question is, what will she choose with me?

She enters the apartment, and sexual tension crackles in the air, but she works to cloak it in small talk, raving about the views of the city, while I flip on the fireplace, and pour her another glass of wine. I join her on the oversized chair near the fireplace and when I would take her wine glass from her, she holds up a finger. "Just one more sip."

Instead, she downs the entire glass. "All done."

"Liquid courage?"

She hands me her glass, which I set on the coffee table. "Courage and nerves are two different things," she says, not really answering my question. I've had courage bred into me and I've learned nerves are not always a bad thing."

"Nerves tell you you're present in the moment," I say, repeating what Kurt apparently taught us both.

"Yes," she agreed. "They do."

I stroke her hair from her face and tilt her face to mine. Fear is not what I see in her face. "You're nervous."

She doesn't look away. She holds my stare and says, "In a good way, Luke."

The way she uses my name, the certainty of her voice, exudes confidence, but it's also her way of letting me know she makes her choices decisively. She's here. She wants to be here. I matter enough to make her nervous, but it's the good nerves, the kind that doesn't cripple but instead excites. I kiss her, savor her, mold her close, a possessive need clawing at me.

My lips part hers, lingering there, a breath from another kiss, the sweet taste of her on my lips, the flowery smell of her teasing my nostrils. I think about her nerves, and while I do believe they are good nerves, they're also about the unexpected, about fear, about the inability to fully trust someone you don't really know—at least, not yet. I find myself craving her trust in the most physical of ways.

I brush my lips over hers again and then stand her up in front of me. "Undress for me, Ana."

It's a power play, I know, but she wouldn't be with me right now if she wanted a man who begged instead of demanded, if she wasn't aroused by the idea of a man who promised her an escape and the pleasure that comes with it and actually delivers it.

"You want me to undress?" she asks, her voice softer now. "Why don't *you* undress first?"

"No."

"Why?"

"It seems I only have so much willpower when it comes to you," I readily confess.

Her eyes widen and then narrow. "It feels more like a power play."

"Because you don't feel like you're in control right now."

"I'm not out of control," she assures me.

"Because you need to be in control." It's not a question.

"Always," she assures me.

My lips curve. "I should have expected that answer. You are Kurt's daughter."

"*Stepdaughter*," she corrects.

"Stepdaughter," I amend and then I get back to the point of control. "Why do you always need to be in control?"

"It's been bred into me."

"Don't you ever just want to let go? To let someone else take responsibility for what comes next?"

"I don't know how to do that," she confesses.

"Try it, right here, right now, with me. This is just you and me, and how much I want you, and I hope you want me."

"I wouldn't be here if I didn't."

"Then just be here, don't think, and don't try and compete. Live in the moment. Undress for me, Ana."

"While you watch."

"Yes. I want to watch. Very much. Will you let me?"

"It feels like a challenge."

"It's not, sweetheart," I say, and I dare to push her. "It's an order. I know you understand those. Step back and undress for me before I lose my fucking mind from wanting you naked."

Her lips curve and she scrapes her bottom lip with her teeth, her hand pressing to my cheek. "Since you put it that way, I was also taught to never disobey a direct order."

CHAPTER THIRTY-SEVEN

Ana

PRESENT DAY...

I'm as nervous as the first night I undressed for Luke, my hands trembling and I don't know why. But then, this is Luke, the man whose ring I wore, the man I intended to marry. Maybe that's the entire point. He *is Luke,* the only man that ever made me feel wholly female, whoever allowed me to be vulnerable without there being regret in the aftermath.

I still to this day don't believe he'd ever intentionally hurt me.

And yet, I feel as if I have no right to be with him, as if I dishonor my brother, but what do I do at this point to make it right? When do I admit that Kasey is responsible for his own demise? When do I just accept, rather than simply speak the fact that I am not whole without Luke?

I can't walk away from Luke and life threw us back together for a reason, and while it might be to stay alive, quite literally, I certainly feel more alive than I have in years just being with him, being challenged by him.

I'm not going to do something foolish like walk away from this night. Or afternoon. Whatever it is right now, with him.

He takes off his boots but I know that's all he's taking off. This isn't my first rodeo with Luke Remington.

I follow his lead and remove my own boots, and then unsnap my pants. The zipper follows before I slide my pants and panties over my hips, giving a little intended shimmy in the process. It all goes down my legs, and soon I'm kicking them aside. After which, I do what I know he expects. I stand there, letting his eyes roam my body freely, which is, in my book, the definition of vulnerability. I'm naked. He is not. He is in control. I am not. Only what I know now, and couldn't know that first night, was the skill Luke has at being my equal and still being a hell of a damn good lover.

His eyes lift to mine and he uses his fingers to motion me forward. Again, *he's* in control. I am not. It's this game we played most of our time together. Kurt demanded I always be in control. And I mostly live that way, unless it's between me and Luke in the most intimate of ways. Letting go with Luke was always a relief. He represents the only time I could ever just be free. He represents the only time I ever trusted anyone completely. And yet, that person, that man that I believed in so completely, killed my brother. He made that decision. In my mind, I know he would never do that if he had other options. In my heart, I hate him not finding that option.

And I love him.

I'm so fucked up. I'm really fucked up. But I'm a better version of fucked up right now with this man about to touch me.

I step forward, following his command, and he watches me move. His eyes are all over me, a touch that isn't a touch. A touch that makes me crave his hands on my body. When I'm in front of him, he looks at me, and then he does what I don't expect.

He presses his hands together, almost as if he's praying, and murmurs, "You're still so damn perfect. Why do you have to be this damn perfect, Ana?"

His voice is fraught with emotion and when normally this is where he wants me to wait to touch him, I don't. My fingers tangle into his hair and I pull his gaze to mine. "Because you want to hate me?"

"Because *you* are always going to hate *me*." His voice rasps with the certainty of his words.

"It's not that simple, Luke. You know that."

"And yet, it is."

I want to tell him he's wrong, but he sits there on the bed, and folds me to him and presses his face to my naked belly, murmuring something I can't understand. Seconds tick by and he just holds me there. And holds me a little longer. I don't know what to say or do, but I don't have to wonder for long. He begins to gently rub the rough stubble of his whiskers against my belly, and of all the things he's done to me, and there is a long list of those things, I think this affects me the most. Not because it's the most erotic or daring, by any measure. No. It's the tenderness, the absolute emotional intensity of the moment that undoes me. We are connected, and yet, we are broken, but somehow whole again, right here, right now.

He turns his head and kisses me and my belly trembles beneath his lips and the tease of his tongue, mixed with the possessive flex of his fingers on my hips. I have never felt more owned, and Luke has done plenty in our intimate moments to own me, of that I cannot deny, nor do I regret one little bit.

His hands curve around my hips, palms exploring my backside before his fingers gently flex into my cheeks. At the same time, his teeth scrape my hip. My fingers tighten in his hair and my sex clenches in anticipation of where his mouth may go next. He knows too, I know he knows. Of course, he knows. The many naughty things I have done with him only became more delicious as he learned about what pleased me, what pushed me, what drove me wild.

Two of his fingers slide down my belly, and oh God, they find my clit, and gently tease me. Heat rushes through my body and he glances up at me and says, "I like it when you get wet for me, Ana. *For me*," he repeats, a rough possessiveness to his tone. "And no one else." He catches my nipple with his lips and suckles me mercilessly, his fingers sliding into my sex at the same moment.

I moan, and it's not a shy moan at all. I *am* wet, so very wet, my body awakened for the first time in years. My hands are now on his shoulders, bracing myself for what comes next. Lord help me, I'm so embarrassingly close to an orgasm. And as usual, he knows this, too, as he abruptly deprives me of his touch. I'm left panting, but not surprised, not one little bit.

Pleasure with Luke is always hard and fast or bittersweet torment.

This time it's the bittersweet torment.

CHAPTER THIRTY-EIGHT

Ana

Luke grabs his phone and turns on a music mix. "For privacy," he murmurs as a song fills the air, soft but present, but I know it's more than what he's claiming. Luke has this thing about blocking out everything but us, and if ever there was a time we needed to do that, deserved to do that, in fact, it's now.

A second later, he folds me close again and stands, lifting me and taking me with him, walking toward the oversized chair in the corner, next to the gas fireplace he turned on earlier. He sets me on the ottoman and claims the chair in front of me, lifting my legs to either side of his hips and then pulling me and the ottoman up to his knees. "Lean back," he orders, but he doesn't wait for my compliance, capturing my hands and pressing them to the cushion behind me, the delicious partial weight of him leaning over me.

He pulls my hips forward slightly, ensuring that I can't move unless he allows me to move, not without falling. We're back to control—his, not mine. But after two long years of desperately seeking control and never finding anything remotely familiar, I don't want it. Not now. Not tonight.

He's still holding my hands down, his mouth hovering over my mouth, lingering a moment before he presses it to mine, a long slide of his tongue seducing me, arousal vibrating through my body. "Ana," he murmurs, as if he just needs to say my name and know I'm really here.

"Luke," I whisper. "Though right now, Lucifer might be more appropriate. You love to torment me."

His lips curve slightly and he nuzzles my neck and whispers, "I do love to torment you." As if proving that to be true, his hands caress a path up my arms and back down until he cups my breasts. He leans in and nips my lips, a pinch that he soothes with his tongue while his fingers tease my nipples.

"Luke," I whisper, my sex clenching, my hips arching toward him.

He answers by lavishing my nipple with delicate kisses, before his teeth tease it, his mouth suckling. He teases me mercilessly, knowing what I really want, knowing where I really need him, until I give him what we both know he wants.

"Please, Luke," I pant out. "Please."

His lips curve again, satisfaction in his deep blue eyes as he presses his lips between my breasts and begins kissing a path downward to the lower expanse of my belly. His mouth remains there, but his fingers find the slick wet heat of my sex, exploring, teasing. When I'm about to plead for sanity, he drags his mouth lower, kissing my clit.

That's when I become aware of the music, and I don't know why. Why now? Why? It's Fletcher's "Undrunk," which is a break-up song. I do not need a break-up song right now.

I drop my arms and fall on my back, and he captures one of my legs, dragging it to his shoulder. The minute he suckles me, his fingers stroking me inside as he does, I moan softly, while the song pushes its way into my mind.

Wish I could get a little undrunk so I could uncall you

At five in the morning, I would unfuck you

I must stiffen or react in some way, because Luke slides his hands under me and lifts me off the cushion, cradling me. "That's not us. That's not what this is. I will not regret this and hope like fuck you won't either."

"No regrets," I promise but in the back of my mind I know—*we both know*—that's easier to say in an intimate, passionate moment.

But there's no more discussion.

His mouth closes down on mine, and I can taste myself on his lips, the intimacy between us exploding, shifting, taking on its own life. We're touching each other, hands everywhere, our kisses almost desperate, as if this is it, our one last chance to be together. At some point, he shoves back the ottoman and stands with me, both of us working his pants. The slow burn is now hard and fast, but not fast enough for either of us.

Finally, I think, when he kicks away his pants, his thick erection at my hip, my hand wrapping it. He groans softly, and it's not a complaint. He catches my waist and sits, taking me with him, pulling me across his lap. I straddle him, his erection between us, his hand on the back of my head, his tongue against my tongue. And he tastes like everything I've ever wanted. He always has.

"I need to be inside you," he murmurs and when he would lift me, I catch his legs with my legs.

"Aren't you even going to ask about birth control?"

His eyes meet mine and he says, "I couldn't give two fucks about birth control." His voice is a low, almost angry rumble, history in its depths, *our* history.

We wanted a horse ranch, and kids, and two dogs, and two cats, a fantasy land in the world we lived in, but we didn't care.

It's another one of those things you can say in the moment, but you might not mean later, but it doesn't matter. I'm still on the pill. Maybe I always hoped this day would come because it sure wasn't for anyone else. He drags my mouth to his, and whispers, "Are you going to say anything?"

"I really need you inside me right now." And this time when he lifts me, I catch his shoulders as he presses inside me, and I pant with the sensation of him sliding deep while I ease down the length of him. My lashes lower, my entire body vibrating with the intensity of what I feel right now that is far from just physical. He is a part of me, and I was incomplete without him.

He is my person and I don't even want to think about how I reconcile that with what is between us. I just want him. Now. Right now.

"God, I missed this," he murmurs, kissing my neck and then cupping my face, and tilting my gaze to his. "So damn badly, Ana." His voice is aroused, emotional, the rough baritone intoxicating.

His hand presses to the center of my shoulder blades molding my breasts to his chest, his mouth coming down on mine as he lifts his hips, and I arch into the movement, moaning against his mouth. We are no longer two people torn apart by life and death, but rather two people holding onto it in each other's arms. The air pulses with our need for one another.

If the music is still playing, I don't hear it—there is the thundering of my heartbeat, the heaviness of our breathing. We rock together, slow and sultry, savoring every moment, his eyes and hands all over me, mine all over him.

But there is a shift between us, a building need between us that is tangible, combustible.

We're moving faster, each meeting of our bodies a thrust and grind. Neither of us are in control now. My fingers tangle in his hair. His catch my nipples, creating a delicious ache in my breasts, in my body. I'm on the edge again, and I desperately don't want to tumble, not yet. I catch his hand, try to slow down, but I can't stop what is already roaring between us, the friction that is our bodies burning for more.

My release rushes over me, out of my control, my sex clenches around him. I bury my face in his neck as my body trembles, shakes. He groans with the impact, pulling me down against him as he lifts his hips and shudders into orgasm. I fade into the sweet release, the ultimate pleasure, but it's inevitable that it must end. I become aware of the music and the room, of his arm wrapped around me a little too tightly, as if he really does believe I will run away. I don't want to run. In fact, I hold onto him, too, trying to beat back reality.

But accepting it is another thing that is inevitable.

The fine line between love and hate between us is real.

The reason we fell apart still exists.

And my confusion over wanting him, hating him, loving him, is just as real.

I don't know how to fix us. We're still broken.

CHAPTER THIRTY-NINE

Lucifer

When I want to hold onto Ana, she is quick to slide off of me, grabbing a tissue which is expected until she says, "Bathroom."

Which is also a thing. She goes to the bathroom after sex. Don't most women? But she doesn't look at me. She also grabs her clothes on the way out of the room, which has me focusing on all of the tension in her spine, not her perfect ass. She enters the bathroom and doesn't shut the door, and yet, a shut door is exactly what I'm feeling right now.

I sit there, seconds ticking by that turn into even more seconds, and then more, waiting on her to return.

Maybe I pushed her too hard, considering all that is between us right now.

But damn it, I needed to know she's all in, I needed to know that she's willing to give herself to me again, to trust me.

The truth is that when I met her, I was a man with a history, a man I didn't want her to ever know, and yet, I couldn't resist getting to know her. She was Kurt's stepdaughter. She knew my world. She knew my nickname, my job, and my past added up to more than how I flew a jet. She demanded the truth from me, extracted all the good and bad parts of me. She knew everything about me.

And she accepted me.

She loved me.

Now, maybe not so much.

The shower turns on, which feels like avoidance. No. Not happening. She will not hide from me. I stand up and I don't bother with my clothes. Sure enough, I find her in the shower. I open the door and join her, pulling her to me.

"What's going on?"

"Nothing." She folds her arms in front of her, almost shyly. Ana is not shy. "I just needed the hot water," she adds.

"What's going on?" I repeat, guiding her out of the flow of water and against the wall.

"I'm fine."

"You're not fine," I insist.

"Wasn't there another way?" she blurts, her voice trembling with emotion. "Couldn't you have shot his leg or his arm?"

My hands fall away from her. "He had a gun to the head of the princess I was escorting to another country. He'd killed three of our men. And I had no idea who was left that was on my side. No. It was him or me and the princess, and she was an innocent, Ana."

She squeezes her eyes shut. "I don't know how to do this, Luke." She opens her eyes. "I don't know how to be without you, but I don't know how to be with you, either. It feels wrong. You killed Kasey."

Realization washes over me as sure as the water pounding at my back. "Is that why you're in the shower? To wash me off of you, Ana? You feel dirty now?" Suddenly needing the hell out of this shower, I turn to exit.

She catches my arm. "No. God, no. I thought I was going to cry. I felt like a silly fool. I didn't want you to see me like that."

"That's not how we operate, Ana. You don't have to be a soldier with me. You know that. That's not us."

"We aren't us right now, Luke."

"That wasn't my choice, Ana."

"I know that. I know I handled my side of things horribly. I didn't mean to shoot you. I swear to you. I would have died with you if you had died. And I was an idiot. I shot his hand. I know better. He could have killed us both. And I know that's your point with Kasey. He could have shot you and the princess, but that doesn't change my guilt. I don't know how to be without you. I don't know how to be with you. But I missed you, Luke."

I draw her to me, and stroke wet hair from her face. "Let's get out of the shower and talk."

"I need to wash and dry my hair. What if we suddenly have to go? But that's not an excuse to avoid talking. I want to talk. I do."

"You want space."

"No. Stay in here with me." She steps into me and wraps her arms around me. "Just be here with me. Let me feel *us* again."

"Except we don't exist anymore. Remember?"

"Not knowing how to fix us doesn't mean I don't want to fix us, Luke."

"Do you?"

"Yes, but I won't lie and tell you that doesn't terrify me more than any enemy I ever faced."

That reply tells me everything I don't want to know. She's not ever going to be able to live with me and the truth. We have now. We have no future. And I'm not sure what to do with that. I'm not sure how to change that. I'm not sure she really wants me to try.

CHAPTER FORTY

Lucifer

I make Ana get dressed and I do the same. Naked isn't exactly a direct path to conversation, not after two years apart. And dressing does not mean in a nightgown or some shit like that, either. Once I've nixed that idea, she dresses in baggy sweats and a tank top, and if she'd paired that with a bra and her nipples weren't puckered beneath the cotton, I'd be a little less distracted. I pull on jeans and a T-shirt. My nipples don't pucker, but my cock damn sure is ready to go again.

That fucker.

Conversation first. Naked next.

The problem is that the barriers between us aren't about sex. They're about life. The one we once shared together.

I sit on the chair where we'd had sex earlier, which isn't necessarily the best location for this conversation, but then neither is the bed. She sits on the ottoman by the fire and gets right to the point. "Just because I don't think you really understand this, and I'm not sure how you could, I never stopped loving you."

It's a good start, if it didn't feel like it has about ten "buts" attached. "I never stopped loving you, but that isn't the real issue here, now is it?"

"No," she agrees. "Obviously not. And it's not even just about you killing Kasey. To be fair to you, at least to some degree, it's also how I handled it."

"Death is unfair, Ana. So is life sometimes."

187

"I did try and call you," she says once again. "You wanted to know when. Not long after the funeral."

That's better than a year later, I think, right about the time I accepted a dangerous overseas mission, the one where I met Adam. "And if I would have answered, would it have changed anything?"

"You wouldn't have spent two years thinking I shot you on purpose."

She's not wrong, but I'm not sure that would have changed much. "When you said you shouldn't have shot Trevor's hand, did you know he was dirty?"

"I did," she says. "The minute he told me you were running illegal packages and you killed three of your men. I didn't tell him that, not then. I had to deal with Kasey's death and your role in that happening. But I tried to find him after you left, and I used my badge and resources to do so. Then, of course, I got word he was killed in a car accident."

"A little strange, don't you think? He disappears and suddenly appears when he's dead? Did you see the body?"

"No, but there were dental records."

"Which can be faked."

"With the right resources, and I found no reason to believe he had those." She changes the subject. "I found something two weeks ago. I'm wondering if it somehow triggered all of this. It was Kasey's birthday and I went through that old suitcase of memories he kept all his life. I found two names and numbers which weren't phone numbers, and they weren't socials. I don't think they were bank accounts either."

"What were the names?"

"Moreau and Dubois, surnames I assume, both French. Do you know them?"

"No," I say easily. "They aren't familiar, but I did run a couple missions to France. They could be connections he made during those trips. What about the numbers?"

"Both were long. I emailed them to myself."

"Once we finish talking, I'll grab a computer and you can log in and get them. What else?"

"I researched the names and numbers from my work computer. I'm just thinking, why would this hitlist emerge now, instead of two years ago? Maybe I triggered it."

"Maybe, and someone coming after you would make sense, yes. But as for what you did spurring the creation of a hitlist makes no sense to me."

"Me neither, but in law enforcement, we know that rarely are things coincidences."

"We'll figure it out, Ana."

"We," she says softly. "It's kind of surreal to hear you say that word."

"Yeah," I agree. "It is."

"You aren't a different man."

"I'm the man I was before you met me."

"You aren't a different man," she repeats. "You were always Lucifer. I knew that."

"Maybe that was the problem."

"No," she says, and then more firmly, she adds, "No. If you heard what I said to Savage and Adam—"

"I did."

"Then you know it's not like that."

"Do I?"

She surprises me by choosing to lean closer and press her hands to my legs. Her touch ignites flames in me and not all of them good. Even if she didn't shoot me on purpose, her anger, her hatred, is a betrayal. "I didn't think you were dirty," she assures me. "I meant it when I said you were my hero, Luke. What you said in the shower, it was true. Me hiding anything from you, including tears, was not us."

"Past tense," I say and I don't touch her despite how fucking much I want to right now.

"Only because it's been two years. And I was honest when I said I'm confused."

"You don't know how to be with the man you supposedly love because I shot your brother who meant to kill me, Ana?"

"Luke—"

"Lucifer, damn it. I'm not hiding behind Luke ever again. Not even for you and before you argue with me, Ana, I'm just living up to the man you believed me to be. Call me inspired." My cellphone rings and I grab it from the table beside us, noting the unknown number. I show it to Ana.

"That's strange," she murmurs.

"Exactly," I answer on speaker. "Who is this?"

"Holy fuck, it's really you."

"Parker," I say, recognizing his voice right away, my eyes meeting Ana's as I say, "Good to hear your voice, man."

"Some dude named Blake left me a message. He told me to call him or you. I wasn't sure what the hell was going on."

"There's a hitlist. Jake is dead."

"Jake. No. Shit. *Jake?*"

"I saw him with my own two eyes. He's gone, man."

"Well shit, man. They came for me. I wasn't sure if Blake was one of them, but bottom line, they came for me. I went underground but I had a shit ton of cameras. I heard a few things."

"What things?" Ana asks.

"Ana," he says. "Hey."

"Hey, Parker. They came for me, too. Luke saved me." I grind my teeth at the name as she asks, "What things?" again.

"They mentioned talking to someone named Darius and then something about a package. And sorry, Ana, but I have to ask: Lucifer, this can't be the same package Kasey was fucking with, right? That was two years ago. That disappeared with Trevor."

Ana's eyes meet mine. "Do you think it is?" she asks.

"We have to assume it is," I say, "because nothing else makes sense. Where are you, Parker?"

"I'm still in Texas. Where are you?"

"How fast can you get to Denver?"

"I know a guy with a plane who can keep me off the radar, but by the time I get to him, it's going to be maybe early morning. Maybe noon."

"Go there. Call me when you arrive. I'll find a connection. Can you send me the recordings?"

"Not safely. That's not my thing."

"I'll set-up a secure link. I need a number to call you back."

"I'll text it to you," he replies.

"Great. I'll have the link in about fifteen minutes. Get the hell out of Texas."

"And come to Denver where it's cold but the heat is burning hot. Same ol' Lucifer," he chuckles, "always walking right into the fire, not out of it, but here I come. Talk soon." He disconnects.

"I'm going to find a computer. Get some rest. We'll leave at daybreak." I stand.

Ana stands with me. "I'm coming with you."

"Get some rest, Ana."

"No. That's not how this works. You don't tell me to sleep and leave me in this room while you handle this. I need to see the recordings. And we need to talk about how to handle Darius and what this package might be."

"Fine," I say tightly. "Come with me."

CHAPTER FORTY-ONE

Ana

Fifteen minutes after Parker made contact, me, Luke, Savage, and Adam are sitting around a table with Blake on video chat. The content of the conversation is creating that safe link for Parker, and I pace the living room as I wait for what seems most important: those who have betrayed us, most specifically, Darius. He had to have set me up the day we were ambushed. I can't get my head around that idea.

"We've got the recordings," Luke calls out to me over his shoulder, and I hurry toward the kitchen island where Blake is still on a Zoom-style chat, and Lucifer is pulling up the audio.

I step beside Luke at the end of the island. Adam and Savage are on either side of us. Luke hits the play button on the soundbite and we all listen. It's a bunch of jumbled voices, but Parker is right. There are a couple of things that stand out:

The images are fuzzy. It's impossible to make out faces, and even if we could, the men are wearing masks.

The men, are in fact, *men* judging by stature and tone of voice.

As far as words that can be deciphered:

Find the package.

Call Darius. Update him.

"It sounds like Darius is important," I say. "I just can't get my head around him being a mastermind. A follower, yes. A mastermind, no."

"Me either," Luke agrees, "but it could be as simple as he's supposed to kill you if he finds you, if they retrieve the package. But keep you alive if not."

"Yes," I say tightly. "I do believe that feels more accurate, but I'd like to think that's not the case."

"I tolerated that dweeb without shooting him, but barely," Savage interjects. "Don't even think for a minute he's not as shitty as a shithouse. He is."

"Agreed," Adam says, offering his simpler, quieter opinion. "He's no one I'd turn my back on."

"I can get him to talk," I offer. "I know I can."

"No," Luke says. "Abso-fucking-lutely not. We just said that we believe he is tasked with killing you, Ana."

"I'm highly trained," I argue. "And this isn't just about me. It's about everyone on the hitlist. I'll set-up a meeting. I have the badass Walker team to watch my back."

"I'll set up a meeting," Luke counters. "You stay the fuck out of this."

I whirl on him. "I'm an FBI agent, trained well above the level my badge requires. I'm not asking your permission."

"I don't give two fucks. If I have to tie you up and keep you here until this is over, you can use your time in captivity to plan my arrest. We both know you want to anyway."

I flinch with that remark. "That's uncalled for. I've been honest about how I feel and what I felt two years ago."

"Yeah well, that's still up for debate. You're not going."

"We need this to end," I reply. "Me talking to Darius is the quickest way to make that happen. I'll call him and have him meet me. And while you might not trust me,

Luke, I trust you. If he tries to kill me and I fail to protect myself, I know you'll keep me alive."

"Come with me," he snaps, grabbing my hand and starting to walk toward the stairs, using his larger size to basically bully me.

There's a part of me that wants to stop that right now and do so in a big way. There's another part that reacts to him touching me, the heat of his palm to mine distractingly right, even if it should be wrong. He cuts down the stairs, not up, and leads me to a second living area with a bar. The minute he halts and turns me to face him, I am ready to explode.

That never happens.

He folds me close, cups my head, and kisses me into submission, which shouldn't be easy. I try not to make it easy on him. I resist. In my mind, at least. My body has a mind of its own, it seems, because I melt like a Hershey's Kiss touched by the sun. I don't just give in to the moment, I kiss the hell out of him, wishing, praying he might taste how much he means to me, how much I never wanted him dead.

When his lips part from mine, his hands settle on my shoulders. "I don't think you understand how terrified I was that I was going to get to Denver too late and you'd be dead. I cannot do that again."

Because he still loves me. I know he said those words to me, but this is more than words. It's actions. It's worry. It's him going over-the-top alpha on me to protect me. I press my hand to his chest. "I know you won't believe me when I say this, but you worrying about me feels bad to you and good to me because I really did miss you, Luke. But you didn't fall in love with me because I was the girl who sat back and let someone else do the hard work."

"Talk to me about those options, Ana, that don't include you risking your life."

"I'm on a hitlist," I remind him. "My life is already on the line. Let's get this behind us and then, then I don't know where that takes us, but it's better than here, right? And before you say a word, I didn't fall in love with you because you shoved me in a corner and made me play the damsel in distress who needed a prince charming."

His jaw clenches and he releases me, giving me his back to walk a few steps, running his fingers through his hair before he turns to face me, hands settling on his hips. "We talk this through. We agree on how and when."

Relief washes over me. "I know we haven't slept, but I think now is better than later. The cover of night. I can call him when we get there and say, meet me now or I'll be gone and I won't be coming back."

He considers me a moment and then says, "Let's go. I'm not going to sleep anyway."

CHAPTER FORTY-TWO

Lucifer

I give Ana a new phone with every Walker contact I trust already programmed inside it. After which, we head back upstairs and rejoin Adam and Savage at the island. Blake is still connected via the laptop on the counter. "She's right," I say. "She needs to call Darius and meet with him."

Savage wiggles his fingers at Adam. "Pay up. I told you she'd win. Just like my wife always does."

Adam slaps a hundred-dollar bill into his hand. "What happened to keeping her safe?" Adam challenges.

I don't explain myself. While I'd rather tie Ana up and keep her safe, she was right. She has a right to fight for her own life. I will never be the man who tries to break her. Even if she breaks me in the process of supporting her. "That's why you two are coming with me," I say, "To protect her. As for the package, it has to be the one that Kasey was holding before I confronted him." I give them a quick rundown of how things went down with Kasey, aware of Ana's energy ticking uncomfortably beside me, but this has to be said. "Trevor disappeared at the same time as that package," I conclude. "Whatever it is, he's the answer. Even if he's really dead, which I'm not convinced he is, if we follow his path, we might find answers."

"I'll dig," Blake offers.

"There were dental records," Ana says. "And Trevor wasn't the mastermind kind of guy."

"All he had to do to act like one, was work for one," Blake counters. "When are you leaving?"

"Now," I say. "Ana wants to call Darius when we get there, take him off guard while it's still dark."

"And meet where?" Blake asks.

"I hope the hotel," Ana says. "There will be security there. If he's still there."

"He is," Blake says, "but we can't be sure he'll offer that option."

"And even if he does," I say, "you cannot agree to go to his room."

"I'm fine with that," Ana confirms.

"So if he doesn't tell you he's at the Ritz," Adam chimes in, "you know him. Where is he likely to suggest you meet?"

"Since he's clearly dirty," she replies, "nowhere I'll agree to, however, if he thinks we're somewhere secluded, I have more of a chance of getting him to talk. The problem is finding a place that meets that criteria and makes him feel safe."

"What will he expect you to want?" Blake asks.

"A semi-private place in public that offers coverage and protection. I need to dictate where and it can't be somewhere anyone expects, obviously. They could be ready for me, whoever 'they' are."

"The Ranch is obvious," I say. "It's your safe zone and it's also booby-trapped and wired with cameras. We'll know what's coming."

"The Ranch will feel like a trap."

"How about the cavern? It's deep on the property one of the buildings used for combat training that connects to a series of caverns. It doesn't feel like it's part of The Ranch. We'll have resources there."

"I don't think he'll go there," she says. "Not after his encounter with Savage and Adam."

"Tell him you dumped us, and me especially," I counter. "Convince him the only place you feel safe is there."

"How about the rear of the store where we met?" she suggests. "It will feel public enough not to feel like a trap to him, secluded enough to feel private. But from our standpoint, there are woods behind the place, where the team could hide."

"No," I say. "You are too exposed there."

"Why don't we just make this simple," Ana says. "I'll tell him I know he's at the Ritz. I followed him. I'll see him in the lobby in five minutes."

"He'll know you have help," I argue.

"But no time to do anything about it," she counters.

"It's the best plan we've got," Blake says. "Let her try. And if that doesn't work, we'll adjust. That's what we do. I'm going to work on Trevor. Hit the road." He disconnects.

I glance at Ana. "I do not like this."

"I know," she says. "But as Blake said. It's the best plan we have."

"Said the five-year-old who hid his peas under a napkin," I say dryly.

"In other words," Savage says, "we go prepared to bust a whole lot of balls. I'm going to load up on big shiny guns and lots of bullets." He heads toward the stairs.

Adam lingers, his eyes meeting mine and while he says nothing, I can almost hear him say, "Or leave her out of it."

If only I could, but as Ana pointed out: she's on a hitlist. And I can't take her right to fight for her life.

CHAPTER FORTY-THREE

Lucifer

Since Ana and I haven't slept, and Savage and Adam have had more rest than the two of us, Savage drives our vehicle, and Ana and I ride with Adam, with the intent of sleeping in the back of the SUV. That means me and Ana in a small space, and the possibility of not tangling up together is pretty much zero unless I sleep sitting up. I decide just to erase the conflict from the get-go. I lay down and take her with me, pulling her in front of me. She doesn't fight me. In fact, she snuggles that pretty little ass of hers against me and refrains from commenting on my instant hard-on. When I fold my arm around her, she covers my hand the way she used to do when we would fall asleep in the bed we shared.

I could lay here and think about her in front of me right now, or her naked with me earlier, or her naked in that shower, all of which hold different nuances, or I can rest. Considering I may well stand between her and death, I force myself to shut my eyes, but my mind starts chasing the past and not in a good way. For a moment, I'm back on that airstrip, relieving the moments before I shot Kasey. I can smell the jet fuel, I can taste the certainty that Kasey is going to shoot me and the princess, most likely in that order. I can feel the cold steel of my weapon at my finger when training and experience takes over, and I pull the trigger. I can almost hear his body hit the ground when that's impossible. The plane's engine was roaring at the time.

And I can feel the heaviness of death in the air as Jake and I bag his body, and those of three other men to take them home to their families. Bodies that rode with us to deliver the princess to her destination. Bodies that rode back with us to the States. Adam cranks up the radio, almost as if he knows how damn much I need something to control my mind. He's a damn Team Six SEAL. If anyone knows mind control, it's him. He probably does know exactly what I need. He's even picked a safe selection of music: old school rock 'n' roll, likely to stir nostalgia in the young and old, but not romance.

The song "Rock You Like A Hurricane" by the Scorpions fills the air, and I listen to those words thinking that's exactly what the woman in my arms did to me and still does right here and now. I shove away that thought by the necessity of resting.

I manage to sleep, but you always know when you're going into a combat situation—and that's what this mission is—that it could be the last sleep you ever enjoy. But it won't be Ana's last. I won't let that happen.

CHAPTER FORTY-FOUR

Ana

It's two-thirty in the morning when we reach Denver. We pull into a gas station and Adam hands the SUV over to us while he joins Savage with a plan to follow us. The Walker team members already in the city are in place at the hotel, ready to offer coverage.

A short while later, Luke pulls us into a spot downtown near the Ritz and offers me his phone. I dial Darius. He answers on the first ring, unaware of his caller's identity. "Agent Sanchez."

"Darius,"

"Ana? Are you okay?"

"I'm fine," I say. "Are you?"

"I'm alive but I'm not going home until I know what's going on. I'm at a hotel. What is going on?"

"Good question. Let's meet."

"Where?"

My mind races and I land on a story involving our boss. "Mike told me you're at the Ritz. I'll meet you in the hotel."

"Mike didn't tell you," he accuses.

"Okay, no. I was at the office when you were dropped off. I followed you."

"Why would you do that?"

"Because those men knew where to find me. That felt really dirty, Darius. We need to talk."

"The gas station two blocks from the hotel in ten minutes." He hangs up.

I grind my teeth with the anger I feel right now. He did set me up, that bastard. "The gas station two blocks away. He hung up, but there's no way he has time that quickly to get backup."

"Whoever he's working for is watching him," Luke says. "You know they're watching him."

"Then thank God you and your team are watching me."

He just stares at me a moment, and I'm sure we're about to fight. Instead, he takes his phone and punches a button. "You got that, Blake?" he asks. A second later he hangs up and it's clear that his phone is monitored at least when it needs to be, because he says, "The team is getting into place. You need to walk. I'll shadow you."

I nod and reach for the door. He catches my arm and pulls me around to him. "I will not let you die."

"Good," I say. "I'd really like the chance to feel what it's like for you not to hate me."

"I don't hate you, Ana. I think the opposite is true."

"I don't hate you, either. Please, no matter what happens, please remember that."

We stare at each other, seconds ticking by before we come together and kiss hard and fast. "I love you, too," he murmurs. "Let's get this over with."

We both slide to our sides of the vehicle, a sense of finality to this that I do not like.

I pull a beanie from my jacket, put it on, and stuff my hair inside before I exit the vehicle, my primary weapon at my side, another in my boot, and in my jacket pocket. I'm aware that I could be followed by someone other than Luke, and I head to the side of a building, entering an alleyway, staying off the main walkways. I know Luke is behind me but I never hear him. I never see him, and I look. I have to look, just in case, there's someone else there. When I bring the gas station into view, I scan the area, confident that I am not alone. Walker Security is a mighty force, and I have a team with me.

Two cars pull to the side of the building and there is safety in numbers. With an adrenaline rush, I walk across the driveway. Walking draws less attention than running. I walk between the two cars. At this point I'm right by the back of the store, but still at the side. I watch the people head to the front of the gas station. I ease around the corner and find Darius pacing. I watch him a moment, his nervous energy like a tennis ball being pinged between a racket and a wall.

I hate how exposed I am once I join him, but he has answers and I'm not the only one on the line. There's a list and I don't even know how long that list might be. I draw a breath and round the corner. The minute he sees me, he rushes toward me, catching my arm, his voice low, urgent. "I have to talk fast." He shoves something in my pocket. "I didn't want to be a part of this, but they threatened my sister. They're powerful."

"So you set me up to die? And what did you just put in my pocket?"

"They weren't going to kill you. They wanted Lucifer. They're looking for some package that they think he has."

"They killed Jake. They were going to kill me. And what package?"

"I don't know, but they offered me a million to help retrieve it."

"Who is they?"

"I don't know. But they're going to call you. Answer."

"You don't have any idea?"

"All I know is there's a powerful man named—"

He never finishes the sentence. He goes down, blood splattering all over me as he does. Darius is dead. Shot dead. I never have the chance to run. Lucifer is there immediately, crowding my body with his body, willing to die for me. He backs me around the corner, and gunfire erupts, most of which seems to be offering us coverage, but I can't be sure. We run and run some more. We don't stop at our car, it's just too close. We're a good mile away when we pause behind another hotel's dumpster. We're leaning there, breathing hard when my pocket rings.

I look at Luke. "Darius put something in my pocket. It must be a phone. They can track us from the phone."

And even as I say the words, I expect that any minute we'll be cornered by men with guns.

***

Lucifer

I push off the dumpster, and hold out my hand. "Let me have the phone."

Ana hands it to me, and I answer the call, already knowing who to expect. The man I spoke to once before. The man who killed Jake. "What do you want?" I ask.

"The package," the man says.

"I don't know what you're talking about."

"And yet, we both know you do. Let. Me. Be. Clear. There are powerful people who want that package. My boss is one of those men. Unless you give it to me in the next twenty-four hours, everyone you have ever known is dead."

My eyes narrow. "I don't have it. I don't know what it is. It must be worth a lot of money for you to be such a drama queen."

"Don't play with me."

"I don't play unless I'm paid. I don't have it, but I'll find it for a price. One million. One week."

It's not what he expects. He's silent a beat that turns into three. That's two too many for him to know what the fuck to do right now. "Two days and I let your people live."

"Then I guess I'll hang up and your very powerful man will kill you for failing him."

"Wait," he says. "Two days and a million dollars."

"A week and two million. I don't know what the fuck it is or where to start looking."

"Five days and one million dollars. And if you go one minute over, I'll kill them all anyway. Don't underestimate me. We're as good as your little Walker team, but we don't play by the rules. Meet me at your little bitch's property, The Ranch. Five days," he repeats. "Don't be late." He disconnects.

If he were as good as he said he is, he'd know his target. He'd know I won't play for pay with the man that killed Jake and threatened Ana. But this works. I bought time to find him and kill him and I will. I hit a few buttons on the phone, text the information on it to Blake, then throw the phone in the trash. That prick won't be contacting me or tracking us. I grab Ana's hand and start running.

THE END...FOR NOW

***

LUCIFER AND ANA RETURN VERY SOON!

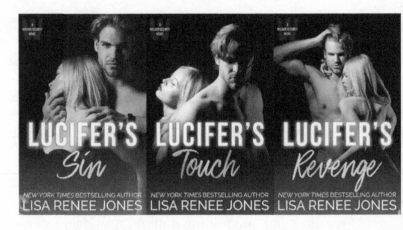

Tall, dark, and deadly, these men run Walker Security. Each is unique in his methods and skills, but all share key similarities. They are passionate about those they love, relentless when fighting for a cause they believe in, and all believe that no case is too hard, no danger too dark. Dedication is what they deliver, results are their reward.

Meet Lucifer, one of those men...

A man with demons that run deep and dark...

The only woman who can bring him to his knees...

As one of the newest members of Walker Security, Lucifer lives up to his name. He's a man with demons that run deep and dark. A man with secrets. A man betrayed by a woman, and that betrayal has shaped every part of his life moving forward.

He lives on the edge with fast cars, faster women, and some might say a death wish. That is until he crossed paths with Walker Security and one of their own pulled him from the bowels of his self-created hell.

But his own personal devil is about to show herself again. That woman from his past is back, and nothing is as it seems.

PRE-ORDER THE REST OF THE TRILOGY HERE
https://www.lisareneejones.com/walker-security-lucifers-trilogy.html

***

AND DON'T MISS THE NEXT BOOK IN THE LILAH LOVE SERIES—HAPPY DEATH DAY!

Kane Mendez.

The son of a drug lord, who is not his father's son, and yet, he has enemies. Too many enemies.

Lilah Love.

The FBI agent who perhaps kills a little too easily. Or does she? As she's called in to consult on a case, and

catch a killer, her troubles back home don't go away
People want her dead. She simply wants them dead first
Kane and Lilah. Lilah and Kane. War is on the
horizon. And everyone won't survive.

FIND OUT MORE ABOUT HAPPY DEATH DAY
HERE:
https://www.lisareneejonesthrillers.com/the-lilah-
love-series.html#HappyDeathDay

***

Don't forget, if you want to be the first to know about
upcoming books, giveaways, sales, and any other
exciting news I have to share please be sure you're
signed up for my newsletter! As an added bonus
everyone receives a free eBook when they sign-up!
http://lisareneejones.com/newsletter-sign-up/

THE NECKLACE TRILOGY

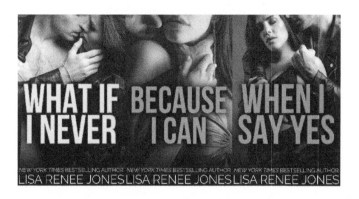

A necklace delivered to the wrong Allison: me. I'm the wrong Allison.

That misplaced gift places a man in my path. A man who instantly consumes me and leads me down a path of dark secrets and intense passion.

Dash Black is a famous, bestselling author, but also a man born into wealth and power. He owns everything around him, every room he enters. He owns me the moment I meet him. He seduces me oh so easily and reveals another side of myself I dared not expose. Until him. Until this intense, wonderful, tormented man shows me another way to live and love. I melt when he kisses me. I shiver when he touches me. And I like when he's in control, especially when I thought I'd never allow anyone that much power over me ever again.

We are two broken people who are somehow whole when we are together, but those secrets—his, and yes, I have mine as well—threaten to shatter all that is right and make it wrong.

FIND OUT MORE ABOUT THE NECKLACE TRILOGY HERE:
https://www.lisareneejones.com/necklace-trilogy.html

ALSO BY LISA RENEE JONES

THE INSIDE OUT SERIES

If I Were You
Being Me
Revealing Us
His Secrets*
Rebecca's Lost Journals
The Master Undone*
My Hunger*
No In Between
My Control*
I Belong to You
All of Me*

THE SECRET LIFE OF AMY BENSEN

Escaping Reality
Infinite Possibilities
Forsaken
Unbroken*

CARELESS WHISPERS

Denial
Demand
Surrender

WHITE LIES

Provocative
Shameless

TALL, DARK & DEADLY / WALKER SECURITY

Hot Secrets
Dangerous Secrets
Beneath the Secrets
Deep Under
Pulled Under
Falling Under
Savage Hunger
Savage Burn
Savage Love
Savage Ending
When He's Dirty
When He's Bad
When He's Wild

LILAH LOVE

Murder Notes
Murder Girl
Love Me Dead
Love Kills
Bloody Vows
Bloody Love
Happy Death Day
The Party's Over

DIRTY RICH

Dirty Rich One Night Stand
Dirty Rich Cinderella Story
Dirty Rich Obsession
Dirty Rich Betrayal
Dirty Rich Cinderella Story: Ever After
Dirty Rich One Night Stand: Two Years Later
Dirty Rich Obsession: All Mine

Dirty Rich Secrets
Dirty Rich Betrayal: Love Me Forever

THE FILTHY TRILOGY

The Bastard
The Princess
The Empire

THE NAKED TRILOGY

One Man
One Woman
Two Together

THE BRILLIANCE TRILOGY

A Reckless Note
A Wicked Song
A Sinful Encore

NECKLACE TRILOGY

What If I Never
Because I Can
When I Say Yes

LUCIFER'S TRILOGY

Lucifer's Sin
Lucifer's Touch
Lucifer's Revenge

*eBook only

ABOUT LISA RENEE JONES

New York Times and *USA Today* bestselling author Lisa Renee Jones writes dark, edgy fiction including the highly acclaimed *Inside Out* series and the crime thriller *The Poet*. Suzanne Todd (producer of Alice in Wonderland and Bad Moms) on the *Inside Out* series *Lisa has created a beautiful, complicated, and sensua world that is filled with intrigue and suspense.*

Prior to publishing, Lisa owned a multi-state staffing agency that was recognized many times by The Austin Business Journal and also praised by the Dallas Women's Magazine. In 1998 Lisa was listed as the #7 growing women-owned business in Entrepreneur Magazine. She lives in Colorado with her husband, a cat that talks too much, and a Golden Retriever who is afraid of trash bags.

Made in United States
North Haven, CT
02 April 2022

17690382R00136